"That was a different life, Patrick, and we've both changed."

"You're probably right." Patrick's voice mellowed, and there was a note of reflection that held Leigh spellbound. "But I hope you don't get the impression that I consider all the changes in you are for the worse...."

Leigh hardly dared to move.

"No, you have changed into a stunningly beautiful woman, and I don't think there's a man living who wouldn't want to make love to you...."

Dear Reader,

Happy New Year! And what better way to start 1996 than with a great selection of Harlequin Romance titles. We've got two wonderful new series for you, as well! We'll take you Back To The Ranch again with Hitched! A year long celebration of cool cowboys, rugged ranchers and the women who tame them! Let Harlequin Romance show you exactly how the West was wooed!

And first up is popular Australian author Margaret Way with *A Faulkner Possession* (#3391). Marsh Faulkner wanted a "trophy" wife, and Roslyn fitted the bill—love didn't enter into it. Though Roslyn was tempted, she couldn't reconcile herself to being just another Faulkner possession....

Every month for a whole year we'll be bringing you some of the world's most eligible men in our Holding Out For A Hero series. They're sexy, they're charming but, best of all, they're single!

This month it's *Husband Material* (#3392) by Emma Goldrick. Though Rose was single through choice, part of her longed for the man of her dreams...a man like Sam Horton, in fact. He was perfect husband material by anyone's standards—despite the fact that he came as a package deal, daughter included!

Also this month look out for:

Passion's Prey (#3394) by Rebecca King. Jared Tremaine was back! Petra had thought she'd seen the last of him ten years ago, but now he was her new neighbor—even more outrageous, even more attractive and even more determined to disrupt her life!

Happy reading and enjoy!

The Editors
Harlequin Romance

Tomorrow's Bride
Alexandra Scott

Harlequin Books

TORONTO • NEW YORK • LONDON
AMSTERDAM • PARIS • SYDNEY • HAMBURG
STOCKHOLM • ATHENS • TOKYO • MILAN
MADRID • WARSAW • BUDAPEST • AUCKLAND

ISBN 0-373-03393-1

TOMORROW'S BRIDE

First North American Publication 1996.

CHAPTER ONE

THE shadowy eyelids flickered briefly, revealing a mere hint of intense violet, drifting closed as she sighed, generous mouth parted on a shudder of sheer anticipation, while at the same time her head moved in what could easily have been a gesture of denial. But it was the teasing, age-old audacity of the born temptress, if the curve of lip or embracing gesture of one slender outflung arm was anything to judge by.

Light curtains stirred at the open window, sending a golden light across the room, gleaming briefly on silky strands of dark hair spilling over the pillow, touching the fringe of dense eyelashes so that she turned from the disturbance in protest, reaching out for a spare pillow, cradling it into the curve of her body as if for protection...

It was a dream she was used to, one she welcomed, had yearned for as it became increasingly elusive. But it had always, as now, come in the mornings, because—and she never doubted it—because it had been their special time. The time when, rested but drowsy, they had taken and given, each to the other, such delight.

Above her she sensed his shape, blotting out that intrusive sliver of light, and she reached for him eagerly, stretching her arms to link them about his neck, offering up her mouth and all the while knowing, with that potent little throb at the pit of her stomach, knowing that in a moment their eyes would meet, would sparkle at each other in such perfect love and understanding, and from time to time with even a hint of amusement and wonder. Yes, always, always wonder.

But the stab of nostalgia was thrust aside; it had been such fun, as well as all those other superlatives which didn't go halfway towards describing their feelings for each other. Such fun and... Another sigh, throbbing and deep, and then, playing by the rules of the game, which didn't always work, she allowed her eyelids to drift apart, and then...

Damn. Damn. *Damn.* A hand went up to cover her eyes and, unable to hide the twist of pain about her mouth, she took a moment or two to regain control. She lay back, eyes closed, expression deliberately blank. You fool, she admonished herself, reverting weakly, when you had so nearly got your life back together again. And all because yesterday you glimpsed someone who reminded you—not even a figure, just the back of a head disappearing into an office. Something about the way the hair lay against the skull, the set of the broad shoulders... for that you suddenly flip your lid, go off on a trip like a junkie in need of a fix.

So what? With one lithe, determined move she left her bed, pausing for a moment to adjust the curtains and fix the window. Gradually over the years she had learned a painful lesson—that self-indulgence was a futile exercise. If she allowed herself to stray along that path, she would never break free, would be permanently inhibited in her dealings with men and——

And quite apart from anything else, she determined to jerk herself back to her usual hard-headed outlook. If she didn't wake up her ideas she would never be fit for what promised to be an excessively busy day, even by her own demanding standards. Even when the work was over, this evening she was expected to attend the reception—the annual shindig organised for so many of those who were employed by the European Parliament here in Strasbourg. Funny, she had been looking forward to it . . . only, suddenly, she wasn't so sure. But right now a shower was needed, something to bring her back to her senses, perhaps even a cold one. She shivered, pushed open the bathroom door and reached bravely for the tap.

Beauty, opulence, unbelievable luxury—those were her first and continuing impressions as she climbed the sweeping staircase, Kyle's hand protectively on her elbow, her mind clicking like a camera recording detail. Glittering chandeliers, gilded balustrades. She was aware of intense appreciation as her eye lingered on classical statues in their shadowy niches, then shock, followed by private amusement, when she identified the glamorous creature approaching from the mirrored alcove.

The effect of fine feathers was amazing. She
wrenched her eyes away, though the image
lingered, and for the first time she excused her
wild extravagance in buying the dress. After all,
it would have been impossible to venture into
such a fairy-tale world in something she had
picked up in a chain-store while at Céline's...

The saleswoman had been right to persuade
her; the colour *was* perfect, the deep blue shades
of the Thai silk *did* enhance the already striking
violet of her eyes, while the tiny velvet bolero
jacket studded with beads and bugles competed
successfully with the glitter of jewels worn by so
many of the more affluent women.

It was the new hairstyle which had caused her
more reservations, but here, in such an ultra-
glamorous location, it looked sensational rather
than extreme, which her good sense told her it
was verging towards. Certainly, it was wildly at
odds with her usual simple styles. But now, approaching the double doors of the reception-
rooms, she straightened her shoulders and raised
her chin as if challenging anyone to remark that
the riot of ebony curls was other than madly
attractive.

As they made their way through the room she
sensed one or two raised eyebrows. Her antennae
picked up approval—even Sir Alan Barclay,
always regarded as something of a cold fish, allowed himself a tiny admiring smile, to which she
found herself beginning to respond.

That was when Kyle diverted her. The smile
was still about her mouth, sparkling mischie-

vously in the wide, brilliant eyes, when she turned, and was instantly stricken to the heart by that dark face, those penetrating...smoky and penetrating eyes and... Reality began to drift away from her, reason to desert her. She was back in her dream; she must be. What other explanation could...?

'Leigh, I don't think you've met Patrick Cavour. He's been here for...what is it, Patrick? About a week?'

'Less than that.' For the first time in years she was hearing that deep voice. Deep and immensely attractive, with the faintest brush of an Irish brogue, it was a voice that from the first had brought weakness to her knees, shivers of sheer delight to the length of her spine and...nothing had changed. Nothing at all. That throb low in her diaphragm, the pressure in her chest were as potent as ever. 'Here in Strasbourg, just three days.'

'Leigh Gregory.' As he spoke Kyle draped a casual arm about her shoulder. 'The most efficient PA in Strasbourg.'

She felt humiliated by the other man's raised eyebrow, curled mouth, that same sensitive mouth which had—— Angrily she caught at her treacherous thoughts, allowing herself to grow increasingly irritated with Kyle, wishing he wouldn't lay it on so thickly. But then she realised it was of Anna he was speaking, introducing her as *his* secretary.

His secretary? Silently she queried that statement, latching desperately on to something to absorb her irritation. Until that very moment she had considered Anna to be *her* secretary, but possibly, in a manner of speaking . . .

No matter. A moment later—and she couldn't understand how it had come about—she and Patrick were on their own, eyes cagily assessing over the rims of glasses. At least, hers were; his were quite blatant in their scrutiny. Almost immediately he spoke, in that soft, tender way that was so . . . Irish. 'So . . . Leigh. How well you look.' The words were spoken in that beguiling lilt so vividly recalled.

'Thank you.' Smile and manner were both brittle as she forced herself to remember to be on her guard. Once before this man had—— 'And you too.' Which was the simple truth as well as a cause for considerable regret, she told herself, in an attempt to damp down her responses. It would have been easier if he hadn't looked just about twice as devastating as her memory of him . . .

It was all too easy for people like her, ordinary people, to be captivated, even to be intimidated, by people like Patrick Cavour. Those who came from backgrounds where casual privilege was taken for granted, from large, close families with servants who were almost invariably devoted— they enjoyed so many niceties which everyone else could only read about.

There was comfort in allowing her dyspeptic recollections full rein, in remembering how the Cavour home had appeared at the end of a long drive, like something out of *Gone with the Wind*.

Inside all had been discreet, tasteful luxury, and then there had been the horses, the dogs with names like Bran and Luath and——

'It's been a long time——' Seeing his lips begin to curve, again she was consumed with fear at her own weakness. Besides, a little shame at such mean thoughts of people who had shown her only kindness had brought colour to her cheeks.

'Yes.' Quite abruptly she cut him off, allowed her attention to roam over the room, coming to rest with some longing on the group where Kyle was entertaining a gaggle of secretaries, Anna among them, with one of his much honed stories. 'Yes.' At last she was able to raise a smile, cool, falsely detached, and with it a carefully judged frown. 'It *was* at Oxford, wasn't it?' Her heart was thumping at her own hypocrisy. 'That we met, I mean?'

From his instantly changed expression she saw that she had caught him on the raw, was perversely filled with regret as she encountered the narrow dark look, the tightened lips, and when he didn't answer she looked about her in an agony of discomfort, though even with her head averted she could feel the cold stare.

'You must forgive me.' Even when he was icily angry, as she had no doubt that he was, there was still this cadence in his voice, and also... She couldn't say what, except that it struck at her most precious and private memories, nudging at secrets which she had determined to keep hidden.

'Forgive?' Her raised eyebrow was mocking, though something in his expression close to disdain made her quail. 'You?' Nervously she looked down into her glass, then flicked back her long lashes, determined to continue her challenge.

'Forgive me, I *was* staring.' There again, a reminiscence which brought a flutter down her backbone, a surge to her nerve-endings, that voice with all its hints of intimacies shared. 'You remind me so strongly of someone I used to know... rather well.'

All her control was slipping now, her cheeks were aflame, and in a way she was glad he had been insensitive enough to remind her of all the times they had——

Her fingernails cut into the palm of her left hand; it took a superhuman effort to summon a smile and she inclined her head faintly, for all the world like a duchess dismissing a footman, but in the second before she turned away she knew a glow of triumph.

None the less, for the rest of what turned out to be an interminable evening, it was impossible to avoid him. Perhaps, she tried to justify things, it was merely that he was so tall. Whenever she raised her head, there he was. And always he was *making* the evening for the bevy of women clustered round him, and it was an inexplicably melancholy fact that each one might easily have been a top model in a glossy magazine. There they all were, signalling interest so madly that if he had ever had any doubts about himself—an unlikely enough possibility—they would have been instantly dispelled and his own high opinion of Patrick Cavour reinforced.

She sipped at her drink rather desperately, longing to be detached but finding it impossible. Of course he was, and always had been, something to look at. At six feet two or three, he was easily the tallest man in the room, and by a margin of light-years the most striking. He had olive skin and dark, almost black eyes, but for that curious little ring of iridescence round the iris, slightly tilted at the outer corners as if, somewhere way back in his ancestry, a bit of the Oriental had slipped in. Well, not that exactly, as she had found out that weekend she had spent with his family in County Wicklow, but there was some romantic nonsense about an ancestor having come ashore when the Armada was scattered.

He had quite the most attractive smile. Stomach-churning. Afraid of that powerful urge deep in her inside, she watched him laugh at something Inés da Silva had said, saw how the dark throat rose from the white collar, noted the appreciative way he was approving her flamboyant looks, and...

Leigh slid the tip of her tongue over dry lips, tried to pretend that the surging beat of her heart had something to do with the heat in the room. Certainly it had nothing to do with jealousy.

But it was undeniable that things took on a still more difficult aspect when she found herself sitting in the passenger seat of his car, being driven back to her flat. Coming downstairs with

Anna, she had found Kyle in a flap because their official car had been delayed, and the chances of a taxi were non-existent. That was when someone who lived near had offered a lift to him and Anna.

'Don't worry about me, Kyle,' Leigh had said. 'I'll pick up the first available cab—there's bound to be one along sooner or later.'

'We're not going to abandon you here on your own, Leigh; I'm sure I can make some arrangement...' And a moment later she had heard him asking Patrick Cavour if he would be kind enough to see her back to her flat, oblivious, or so it had seemed, to her protesting asides and her simmering resentment.

'Thank you.' When they drew up at the block of flats where she lived he opened the door, patient as she dealt with layers of skirt and petticoats, though she would have seen that his eyes were sardonic if she had chosen to observe them in the pale light of street-lamps. 'I'm perfectly all right now.'

'Nevertheless, I should prefer to see you safely inside.'

Her heels tapped angrily, and even the stir and rustle of silk should have been giving him a message as she swept towards the lift, her mind frantic with one question. *Must* she ask...? At her door they paused, he intent as ever as he watched her slide the key into the lock, and she decided that she must. 'If you would like some coffee...?' Instantly she was shamed by the grudging tone, which he was bound to pick up.

'What?' Mocking disdain. 'Do you mean there's a café on the corner?' It was so apt, so disingenuous that she flushed guiltily, tried to make amends.

'What I *was* going to say was that it would take only a few minutes, if you——'

'*Is* that what you were going to say?' The gleam of white teeth was a mark of lofty disbelief, but at the same time the spark of anger was unmistakable. 'Only——' he pushed back his cuff '—time is getting on, and I hope you won't be *too* disappointed if I refuse. You see, I'm catching a flight for New York in about two hours, and have just enough time to go back to my hotel and change. But——' his faint bow was blatantly derisive '—I want you to know how much I appreciate your offer.' His arm came out, the hand resting on the wall above her head, and he loomed over her in that predatory way men had so that she knew he was going to kiss her.

So what? It happened all the time and meant exactly nothing. She had long ago learned to switch off; she and romance were so mutually estranged that it was easy, and just because he was the one who had taught her all she knew on the subject, it didn't mean she would succumb. In fact she almost welcomed the opportunity to let him know how little she felt, how totally outside his power she——

'Goodnight, Miss Gregory.' He straightened up suddenly—so suddenly that for a moment she wondered, quite seriously, if he had been reading her mind, so unexpectedly that she felt a moment's resentment that he should take such an unfair advantage.

'Wh-what?'

'Goodnight. I must be going, so don't try to detain me...' There he was again, trying to have the last word...

She smiled brilliantly—what else was there for her to do? And she was relieved, after all. 'Goodnight, and thank you.' She had no intention of showing how taken aback she was and yet... perversely she was swept with a sense of regret. After all, he had once been her life... nearly every woman she knew would have given her eye-teeth for just such an opportunity.

Who could blame them? Standing where she was now, it could only reinforce her earlier opinion that he was the very attractive man he had always been—the scatter of silver at the temples merely added to his appeal. She had the notion that he would go grey very quickly, like his father, she remembered. Silver hair combined with such dark, forceful looks would be quite devast——

About to leave, he turned back suddenly, making her start nervously. 'Oh, and Leigh.' She had an idea that the Christian name was a mistake; he had meant to be more formal. 'I take back what I said. That girl I spoke of earlier—I see now the resemblance was an illusion. You're really nothing at all like her.'

His intention to wound was clear—and hadn't she herself handed him the weapon? Staring up into a face that was so cool and detached, she refused to allow him to know exactly how much it hurt.

'Goodnight.' Casually he turned away from her.

She saw him disappear into the lift as she went into her flat, slipping the bolt into position by sheer instinct, reaching the bedroom before the first sob burst from her chest; then, careless of her beautiful dress, she threw herself across the room and face down on to the bed, allowing the tears to stream down her cheeks on to the pillow.

At last they were spent. Exhausted, she turned, went to the bathroom to bathe her burning cheeks, hopelessly got out of her finery and into her nightdress, in the soothing dark with nothing but her own thoughts to disturb her. Because— she had to face facts—for years she had been living in her fool's paradise telling herself she was over it all, congratulating herself on her resilience, but one brief meeting and all that was swept aside.

One thing had been proved to her conclusively: he had been then, was now, and would be to the end of her life, her only real love. Her first and her last. No matter how bitter she felt towards him, there was no escaping that simple fact, no sense in denying the sheer magic of the short time they had spent together.

It had been her last term at Oxford when they had first met, though neither of them could explain how they had missed each other for so long. It could have been her fault, though it was a painful confession. Scraping along on a scholarship, she had been under such pressure to get a decent degree that her social life had been restricted until the finals were out of the way. But when they had met at Deborah Fleetham's twenty-first birthday party, a loud and slightly drunken affair, the attraction between them had been immediate and consuming.

'Tell me about yourself.' Always she had been responsive to voices, and the mellow mid-Atlantic accent was in itself a powerful sexual instrument, especially when used in that imperative style. Add to that the looks of the man, the easy, powerful physique, and any resistance, any sense of discretion simply went.

'Not a lot to tell.' Her last few shreds of caution slipped from her fingers. 'Leigh Gregory, twenty, reading English and history.' She guyed a TV quiz programme popular at the time.

'And where do you come from, Leigh Gregory? And——' reaching out to a passing tray of drinks, he expertly captured two glasses, one of which he handed to her '—more important——' as the red wine touched his tongue he grimaced a little '—where are you going?'

'Going?' She shrugged, pursed her lips. 'Who can say? But I come from a little village in Gloucester. My father's the vicar.' She sipped cautiously, for the first time regretting her lack of experience with alcohol and the confidence it appeared to confer. Even the appearance of sophistication would have been a great advantage in dealing with a man like this, older and so obviously experienced. 'But tell me about you. Apart from your name, I'm completely in the dark.'

'I'm from County Wicklow. After Trinity I went to Harvard Law, then I was with a firm of attorneys in Washington for a few years. I've been here for the past few months doing research, and also to please my father, who was here thirty years ago. You know how fathers are.'

At that she smiled, knowing that this man, with his air of confident affluence, would have an experience at odds with her own. Her scholarly father was so immersed in the study of obscure crumbling manuscripts that he seemed barely aware of his daughter's existence, while her mother... well, she, perhaps forced by boredom or neglect, had taken to enjoying poor health and making unjustified demands on her daughter.

'And explain to me——' Patrick Cavour put a hand on her elbow, guiding her in the direction of a more secluded corner '—just where you've been hiding yourself for the past few months.' He smiled down at her, unaware that simultaneously her insides turned to water, his glance narrowing as it took in the tumble of fine dark hair, the wide mouth, the vividly expressive eyes; then he bent his head and kissed her. 'While I've been searching for you.' His action and words caused a positive ferment of emotions.

The impact was devastating, overwhelming them both with that first contact, so that from then on being apart was exquisite torture; being together was the sole purpose of their lives. When he asked her to move in with him there was nothing to consider. Blithely she embarked on a course which just days earlier she would have considered both risky and quite irrational.

On the day they held their own private ceremony, just the two of them, dedicating their lives to each other—at least that was how she saw it at the time. They exchanged gifts which she thought of as pledges, his a slender Victorian chain, beautifully wrought in silver filigree, supporting a gleaming crystal in the shape of a tear. Long afterwards she wondered if that had been an omen, a warning of all the tears the relationship would bring her, but she had never been superstitious. Even with something as notoriously unlucky as an opal she would have had no sense of foreboding.

As if it were yesterday she could recall each detail of the day. She was checking on her appearance, pleased with the hyacinth-blue dress, with the elegant fitted line and low neck, when he came up behind her, so tall and distinguished, dressed formally for the occasion in a dark suit, his white shirt emphasising his tanned good looks and the pink rose suggesting that there was something quite special in the planned celebration.

As their eyes met in the glass her heart was all at once beating fiercely, then one of his hands was circling her neck, touching her cheek, turning her to face him. He looked at her with great intensity before bending to put his mouth on hers. A moment later she felt the cool metal touch her

skin, looked back at the glass then raised the
crystal to her lips.

'Thank you.' She was unexpectedly shy.
'Thank you, Patrick. It's beautiful.'

'With this silver chain I thee worship.' There
was a thread of amusement beneath the main impression of firm purpose and integrity. 'I wonder
if you know how much I love you? It's so hard
for me to tell you.'

'I think...' She shook her head, mystified by
the sheer power and depth of her emotions. 'I
think I know exactly how much.' And the kiss
they shared was passionate and impatient and
tender, a clear demonstration of mutual need and
dependence.

They had dinner in a country hotel, where after
they had eaten they could dance, but that plan
was defeated by their impatience. After drifting
round once or twice while the band played
smoochy music they found they could wait no
longer. They went back to his flat, and he swept
her up in his arms and carried her inside.

Nothing in her life had prepared her for that
idyllic time spent with him, so short in spite of
her conviction that it would last forever. Magical
delight, intoxication and passion, which on the
one hand had her soaring up to the stars and on
the other brought so much warm laughter, so
many shared interests—perfect friendship.

Her gift to him, a slim volume of love poems,
a first edition picked up in one of Oxford's
second-hand book-dealers, was something he re-
ceived with awe, passing his fingers over the faded

limp leather, over the worn gilt lettering, as if it were the rarest treasure.

And both gifts brought laughter as well as pleasure. She lost count in the days ahead of the times he teased her, laughing at her blushes when he told her that their gifts were the only things they wore in bed.

Now, with the tears aching at the back of her eyes, it was so easy to remember how she had giggled. And blushed. How they had made love. And read the sonnets aloud to each other. How they had done all the silly little things which lovers had always done, and all the while she had been dreaming of, if not actually planning, the day when it would end with all the protocol of a wedding in the church where she had been baptised, surrounded by friends and relatives from both families. And that was one of the things which had made it so difficult to believe when it had ended so abruptly in bitter recrimination.

Recollection of that day was burned into her soul, deeply etched with acid. Having met one of her professors in college, she had come into the flat, bursting with the good news she had been so anxious to share with Patrick. She had opened the door just as he put down the telephone and he had turned, and his face had lit up as it always did with the pleasure of seeing her. She could recall each detail with perfect clarity. He had been doing some work at home, and was dressed in pale chinos and a checked shirt, but somehow he had always maintained an immaculate ap-

pearance, unlike so many of the men she knew—
professors and tutors just as much as students.

'Good news, darling...' And he had held wide
his arms.

'Oh, Patrick. And I have too.' She had run
forward, her mouth to his, revelling in the
pressure of his body against hers. 'But mine will
keep... You first...'

'They want me to go to Ashala for three
years—help set up a large relief project.'

'What?' She frowned, her mind still unfo-
cused, but clearly she was misunderstanding.
'What on earth do you mean, Patrick?'

'You're surprised, of course you are.' His arms
were about her slender waist, pulling her still
closer into the curve of his body, and he was
rubbing his chin on the crown of her head. 'I've
been hoping it might be a possibility but I didn't
want to say until I heard something definite,
and——'

'Ashala, did you say?' She pulled back, staring
up into his face for elucidation. 'Where on earth
is that?'

'It's in Bangladesh, with some of——'

'Bangladesh?' Now panic and indignation were
threatening to run out of control. 'But...haven't
you always said...? I thought you meant to
practise in London. Or Dublin, you said.'

'Eventually, that's on the cards.' Some of her
feelings were clearly reaching him, for his arms
slackened. 'Only this is what I'm going to do

first.' Later she recalled how implacable he had sounded.

'Go to Bangladesh?' At the time—inexplicably, she confessed in retrospect—it had seemed incredible and even slightly ludicrous. 'Am I to understand, then, that highly trained western lawyers are in demand there? For heaven's sake!' she added scathingly, aware of little but the desperate need to change his mind.

'It's not as a lawyer I'm going, though I doubt if the training will be a handicap. I'll be going as administrator for the aid agency and to do whatever is needed. I'm as capable of digging ditches and building huts as the next man, if that's what I find is needed when I get there.'

'But why, Patrick?' She pulled herself away from him. 'That's what I can't understand.'

'Why?' His eyes narrowed as he watched her walk across the room, return with her arms wrapped about her body in a despairing, hopeless kind of way. 'Because I feel I want to put something back, for God's sake. Surely that's easy enough to understand...?'

'No, I'm sorry, but I just can't see it.'

'So all those times when you've reminded me how privileged I've been all my life, when you've enjoyed all those little digs at my expense——'

'Those were——' Aware of handling things badly, she still found it impossible to adapt. 'Those were quite simply jokes—you know they were.'

'Jokes,' he agreed grimly. 'But none the less true. I know how incredibly lucky I've been, and now I think it's my turn to try to help other people, if that doesn't sound too incredibly pompous.'

'*You* said it.' The words were out before she could stop them, and at once she was overcome with a shame which made her long to deny them. 'Oh, I'm sorry.' She raked a distracted hand through her hair. 'Of course I didn't mean it.'

'No?' His expression was impassive, detached in a way that struck terror into her heart, brought her back to the core of her need: the determination to change his mind.

'But there's so much to be done in this country if you have a social conscience.'

'We're not talking about a social conscience. We're talking about a part of the world where there is real, desperate need, Leigh. Don't forget I've seen a fair amount of that in South America, and Bangladesh is one of the poorest countries in the world.'

'But——' her voice was thick with unshed tears '—but what about me?' This was the bottom line. 'What about me?'

'Oh, you silly little fool.' Quite miraculously his face cleared. With two steps he had crossed to her, his arms were about her again, swinging her above the ground, and his voice held relief. 'Surely you didn't imagine...? Or maybe you did, because stupidly I didn't explain properly. You don't imagine I'm going to leave you here, do you? You're coming with me, of course. We're both going to Bangladesh.'

For just a few minutes it was possible to rest there, head above his heart, dreaming, pretending, however briefly, that what he was suggesting was possible. But then, wearily, she had to pull herself away, distance herself from his power. 'But what makes you think, Patrick— what possible grounds do you have for thinking— that I have the slightest intention of going to Bangladesh?'

For a long time he stood there, arms at his sides, simply challenging her, while she could hardly bear to look into his face. 'Because I want you?' he suggested quietly in the end. Then, since she showed no sign of answering, he went on, 'Can't you see, Leigh, what a worthwhile thing it would be for us to do this together? After all, I'm not the only one who has had advantages— every one of us here has privileges most people can only dream of... I'm *asking* you to come with me, Leigh.'

At that moment there was something authoritarian about him, almost paternal, as if he had little doubt that in the end he would compel her to concede. She turned away before her judgement could be swayed, walked into their bedroom and began to hang away some blouses she had ironed earlier, very aware that he had followed, was lounging in the doorway, intent and determined.

'I'm not coming, Patrick.' She spoke before glancing across at him, knowing how much more difficult it would be to refuse if he wore a certain very persuasive expression, then made a great play of adjusting a silk blouse on its hanger. 'And even if I wanted to it would be impossible for me to go so far with my mother's health as it is.' As she had known it would, this remark caused him to sigh heavily and, possibly because it was such a predictable response, she chose to see it as a deliberate slight against her mother, ignoring the reality of the problem which they had discussed many times and from every angle. 'Oh, yes.' Did her voice perhaps sound the least bit querulous? 'It's all right for you. It must be wonderful never to have known——'

'You know what I think about that.' Which was undeniable, as was the fact that for much of the time they had been in total agreement that many of her mother's illnesses were, if not entirely imaginary, certainly less serious than she liked to pretend, and likely to evaporate completely if something came along to tempt her from them.

'Yes. I do know what you think.'

'Your mother has your father with her. It would be quite different if she were on her own.'

'You don't understand.' The unfairness of it all struck at her. 'How could you have any idea what it's like to be an only child? But anyway, this is all beside the point because I'm not going to Bangladesh—in the first case because I'm convinced I'd be nothing but an encumbrance, and in the second...' Her voice wobbled as the spectre of a future without him wavered in front of her eyes; white teeth caught at her lower lip as she forced herself to go on. 'I... notice you aren't showing a great deal of interest in my piece of news.'

'No, I'm sorry. I was about to ask you about that.'

'I told you, didn't I, that Dr Acheson said he'd heard of something which might suit me? Well, it's a post for a researcher at Westminster, and if I want it the job's mine. I just met him and he told me. Naturally I assured him it's exactly what I want. It's as simple as that.'

'Is it?' All at once his nerves, his patience were beginning to show signs of wear and tear. 'And what if I beg you to come with me? If I tell you it won't be at all the same without you, that it's an experience we ought to share together, something as worthwhile, as tremendous as this? It's something we'll remember for the rest of our lives, light-years away from a dogsbody doing tinpot research in the House of Commons.'

The silence as they stared at each other seemed endless. Each of them was angry, desperate with misery, disappointed that the other could be so wrong, determined not to be the one to give way. When at last Leigh spoke she made no effort to hide her weariness. 'I think that just about says it all, don't you? What to me is a wonderful opportunity is nothing at all to you. You couldn't have been more dismissive if I'd said I was going to work on a supermarket check-out.' Her hurt and mortification grew. 'All right, you go off to Bangladesh if you must, ease your social conscience in any way that seems appropriate to you, only, don't expect me to stand quietly on the sidelines while you satisfy your burning ambitions.'

Recollection of those precise words caused more than a touch of shame and embarrassment when she had cooled down. She hadn't meant them, and taken purely at face value they could have indicated, to anyone who didn't know her, that was, that her own ego was in dominant mood...

And Patrick, too, had an opinion about that. It was obvious in the narrowing of his dark eyes as well as in his stony expression, in the tightness of his jaw and lips. 'You're not hinting, are you, Leigh, that I'm off on some kind of self-serving jaunt? If that is in your mind, then...' His shrug was a mark of contempt which made her shrink. 'And as for the idea that you might stand quietly on the sidelines... I have far too much respect for you to think along those lines. You're not the kind of woman I would ever see simply as an adjunct.' In spite of all the contrary indications his voice was light, just a tiny undertow of steel recognisable to someone who knew him as she did. 'So in that respect you could hardly have got it more wrong. Not that it matters now. Not in the very least.'

He turned away just then; she heard his quick footsteps in the adjoining room, and a moment's silence. Silence, that was, except for the agitated hammering of her heart against her ribcage, then the slamming of the outside door. For a long time she just stood there, enduring her misery, then she slumped into a chair and wept.

It was a particular twist of malicious fate which brought a telephone call from her mother later that afternoon, her tone of resignation somehow much more frightening than her more usual dramatic diagnoses as she described the small lump on her neck and the doctor's insistence on immediate investigation.

'So I'm wondering, Leigh, if you can possibly come down and keep Daddy company for a few days. Anyway, here he is now to have a word.'

And of course there was nothing to consider; she had no choice but to go home when the outlook was so fraught.

She could never explain afterwards why she was so devious with Patrick when she told him about it—most likely she was still smarting from his decision and wanted to get back at him. In any event, her deliberately casual explanation elicited only lofty disdain, coupled with what she interpreted as insincere insistence that of course she must go since her mother was ill, both of which increased her simmering indignation.

On the second day of her visit to Great Whencote the result of the biopsy brought overwhelming relief. The lump was a benign cyst and was scheduled for removal within the next month.

'Thank heaven for that.' Her father put down the telephone and turned to his daughter with an uncharacteristic grin. 'It's been such a worry. And now——' he crossed the room and put an arm

round Leigh's shoulder, squeezed it in an unusual demonstration of emotion '—now there's
nothing to prevent you going back to Oxford and
that young man you're so fond of.'

'Father.' She couldn't quite control the colour
which rose so suddenly in her cheeks, and she
grinned in acknowledgement. 'I don't have to
dash away. I'll wait as long as you need me.'

'Well, what I'm saying is, now that the pressure
is off, there's no reason why you should stay here
right now. I know there will be lots going on back
at college, and your mother and I can manage
perfectly well now we know there's nothing
serious. And, as well . . .' He hesitated, then went
on, 'Your mother is inclined to fuss about her
health. To be honest, she's not altogether cut out
to be a vicar's wife. As you know, I was teaching
in a prep school when we met, and I think that
life might have suited her best. What I want you
to know, Leigh, is that you mustn't be too ready
to drop everything when she rings with some
complaint or other. You have your own life and
I don't want that to be sacrificed to us. You
understand what I'm trying to tell you?'

'Yes, I think so.' He hadn't used the word
hypochondriac, but she knew what he meant. On
impulse she reached up and kissed his cheek.
'And thank you, Dad. Only, I want you to
promise that if things ever get really serious you'll
call me. I'll stay now, in any case.'

She made the deliberate decision to let her
anger with Patrick, and maybe even his with her,
cool down for a few days. It might be good for

both of them to miss each other and for them—
for him especially—to reflect on the unfairness
of his decision and how adversely it was bound
to affect both their lives.

Looking back on it afterwards, she was
stunned by her own self-assurance. Crass self-
delusion was a more apt description, she decided, for certainly then she had been wholly
confident that things could be mended in line
with her own inclinations.

But, unbelievably, that had been the end.

Now, lying in bed in Strasbourg, Leigh turned
restlessly, unwilling to relive the final agony of
that time. Right up to the end she had believed,
had even prayed for him to come to her and say
that he had changed his mind. But as the days
had passed she'd found her convictions shaken.
The London job had begun to lose a little of its
glossy image and it had been an immense effort
to stick to her decision. If he had come dashing
up to Gloucester in an attempt at persuasion she
was by no means convinced of how she would
have reacted.

Then with relief, at last, she'd travelled back
to Oxford, her mind fizzing with all kinds of
contingency plans, had gone up to the flat
and...found that he had gone. A friendly, civi-
lised little note had assured her that there was no
need to hurry to vacate since the rent was paid
for three full months ahead, that his date had
been brought forward and that he had just
enough time to see his family before setting off
for New York and the briefing by the aid organ-

isation. All very friendly and entirely soul-destroying, especially the part assuring her that he would always have the happiest memories of the time they had spent together. There was certainly no sign that he was sharing any of her anguish, no indication that he was even missing her.

Twice, pride in tatters, she lifted the telephone in the flat to ring him at his home. Twice she replaced the receiver as she struggled to find the right words for such an occasion, not for the first time doubting the practical use of all her years of study. Each time her courage failed. She couldn't bring herself to do what her instinct demanded, to speak to him, beg him to find a place for her on his team. Anything, she wanted to say. I don't care what it is so long as we can be together.

Then, at last, she considered she was word-perfect. She dialled the number and found herself talking to his sister, Grainne, who was more than willing to have a long chat, and who told her it was such a pity that she hadn't called just a few hours earlier since Patrick was due to be taking off from Shannon about now for his journey to the States.

Her only choice then, she realised, was to find his address and write to him. It might be possible to join the project a little later, and in the meantime, though the idea was much less cheering than she would have imagined earlier, she could gain a few months' experience in the Commons job. Perhaps it was a moment for independence, if only to demonstrate that she could manage on her own. Anyway, she thought, trying to make a virtue out of necessity, this way would be less humiliating, less frantic.

And there was little doubt that, but for a chance meeting with Deborah Fleetham in the supermarket, one day the letter would have been sent.

For Debbie had news which she was more than anxious to impart. It was about her friend who was a nurse at the John Radcliffe. 'You must remember Gillian. You would have met her at my twenty-first—the tall blonde with the marvellous figure. I thought you might have heard ...' The wide, knowing eyes were eager for Leigh's reaction. 'She's off to Bangladesh with Patrick Cavour; they must be in New York by this time. It's all so exciting and romantic, don't you think?'

Only she never did hear what Leigh thought, for Leigh remembered very suddenly about an urgent message, turning away quickly so that Deborah would not see the tell-tale brilliance in her eyes.

Unhappiness she had expected, had been prepared for, in a way, but the physical pain had come as a total shock, she recalled now. She had lost weight, become exhausted with the sheer effort of trying to carry on as usual. It was an experience she remembered with something close to terror, and one she had no intention of repeating.

CHAPTER TWO

WHEN the tall figure swung his briefcase on to the seat beside her, Leigh, preparing for a much needed rest, glanced up in reproach at his intrusion into what she had been hoping was her space, registered someone stowing a grip in the overhead locker, then had to do a swift retake. Her eyes widened in dismay and shock, but the embossed initials on the brown document case, PJC, merely confirmed the message that her brain was determined to reject. Damn. Damn. *Damn*. Nervous irritation was loud in her voice before she had the wit to attempt a disguise.

'What on earth are you doing here?' No use hoping the shrewish note would be missed.

'Much the same as you, I expect.' If Patrick Cavour was rattled by her manner then he was much too cool and experienced an operator to let it show. But still, she could detect wariness in the way his eyes swept over her before he settled into his seat, wariness and something she liked even less—detachment verging towards dislike, or possibly just disapproval. Whatever, it was quite enough to have her nerves screaming as, from the corner of her eye, she saw the long fingers dangerously close, searching for the safety buckle and... She caught a whiff of the distinctive cologne which made the years simply evaporate. Unexpected tears stung; she found herself holding her breath, fascinated by the smooth brown skin, the scatter of dark hair across the knuckles, the heavy gold watch beneath the dazzling white cuff...

'Flying to Paris.' The words brought her from her musings. 'On business.'

Oh, no. Metaphorically Leigh closed her eyes. Surely it couldn't be? It mustn't be... Please God, she began to pray, but without much hope.

'And of course——' the sugary sweetness, the blatant sarcasm, owing so much to sheer terror, were very much misguided, and she regretted them almost immediately '—it *is* mere coincidence that you happen to find yourself in the seat next to mine.'

'No.' His voice lowered conspiratorially as the plane's engines fired. 'I had to bribe Air France—what do you think?' She had been forced to incline her head to catch his words and now pulled back, stung and humiliated, her blazing cheeks indicating how much.

If I were to tell you what I really think... But this time the words were held back and she even found herself smiling ruefully, wondering why she had made it so easy for him... The smile faded; she must be careful—it would be dangerous to allow herself to mellow...

Resolutely she turned her face towards the runway lights now flashing past, her mind focusing instead on the dream, back last night with a vengeance, torturing her with all its blatant erotic images. Sighing shakily with more than a hint of anguish, she pressed her eyes closed, willing sleep...

'Can I persuade you to have a drink?' Naturally, he *would* choose the exact minute when she might have drifted off, but he was impervious to her look of reproof, and when she saw the attendant with the drinks trolley waiting for the order there was no choice but to try to look bright and intelligent.

'What? Oh, no, thanks.'

'Oh, go *on*.' His manner was benign, very nearly indulgent. 'To show you're not going to continue with this silly pretence that you don't remember me. After all, it's not so very long since we were——'

'All right.' It seemed sensible to cut him off before he became specific, especially with the stewardess finding the conversation so intriguing, and apart from that she had had time to reflect on her behaviour the other night. What had seemed clever then, under the influence of shock and more champagne than was good for her, was, in the cold light of morning, merely childish. 'I admit, I knew you at once. You haven't changed all that much.' And only for the better, a treacherous internal voice was determined to observe.

'Thanks,' he said drily. 'Am I right, then, in presuming that an armistice has been declared?'

Her slender raised eyebrow must have been taken for agreement; she heard him order wine as she reached for her handbag.

'You must let me pay,' she said touchily.

'Forget it. You're not costing me a sou.' Something about the offhand way he spoke was wounding. 'It'll all go on my expenses.'

'And of course we all know how lavish they can be.'

'Well——' he gave her a slanted sideways glance '—if you're talking about the Strasbourg set-up, you'll know more about those than I do. And if you insist——' now there was a touch of impatience in his tone '—you can pay next time.'

There is not going to be a next time, she thought as she sipped the cool white wine appreciatively. Then the import of what he had said percolated. 'And why should I know more about these things than you do? Surely someone in your position...?'

'My position?' When he turned to her there was more in his expression than in the words themselves, enough certainly to make her heart behave in a silly rushing way that she could only deplore. 'But tell me, Leigh, what exactly is "my position" as you see it?'

For a long time there was silence while she considered, then at last had to confess that she had no idea. Such had been the panic caused by his reappearance that she had not actually faced that aspect directly. Possibly she might have picked up the impression—something to do with the odd remark she had heard in the office, one or two hints from Kyle—that he had landed a job with the Irish representatives at Strasbourg. He was not an MEP himself—if he had been she was certain to have known—but... 'I'm...I'm not sure,' she confessed at last. 'Legal adviser in some capacity, I suppose.'

'That could be claimed for anyone employed in the legal profession, but I'm certainly not working for any section in the parliament.'

'Oh.' It took her a moment or two to absorb the implications of this. 'Then what?'

'I've been doing some private lobbying on behalf of one of the major aid agencies.'

'Oh...' It was hard to work out why this should be such a shock—not a disappointment, but... 'So... am I to conclude you're still working in that field?'

'No.' His frown suggested that her slowness was an irritant. 'I've got my own international law practice, but because I've had experience I decided to do some of the initial approaching myself.'

This time there was no hiding from herself the fact that she was disappointed. It wasn't—surely it couldn't be—that somewhere, deep at the back of her mind, she had been cherishing the thought that his arrival in Strasbourg had been triggered off... No. Of course it wasn't that. What a relief to be able to dismiss the thought for the utter nonsense that it was.

The arrival of the stewardess with coffee and sandwiches was a diversion, and, although she and Patrick refused, the tall, willowy blonde seemed most reluctant to move on; it was only the obvious impatience of another passenger which dragged her from his side. Leigh, observing the little by-play, was quickly forced to adjust her expression of cynical amusement when he turned to make a routine enquiry about the wine.

'Fine, yes, it's fine.' But her mind wasn't on that; she was intrigued by what he had told her, and she heard her voice before she thought to curb her curiosity. 'So... international law. Does that mean you're living...?'

'Right here in Paris.' He gestured to the city lights over which they had just begun to descend. 'Been here about eighteen months now. But what about you? Are you here on business, or is it pleasure?'

'Both.' She sipped her wine, trying to decide just how far she ought to take him into her confidence. 'In fact for the last few months I've been spending as much of my time in Paris as in Strasbourg. You see, Kyle has extensive business interests and I'm trying to dovetail the two spheres. At first I was a bit reluctant to take on the additional responsibilities, but now I find I'm enjoying it. There's even the chance that the experience might come in useful if ever I decide to change jobs.'

'Oh, is there a chance of that?'

'No.' She shook her head. 'Not right now, anyway, but there are times when the political scene can be... well, I suppose boring would be the most honest description.'

'Mmm.' At least he hadn't jumped in with, I told you so. Then, 'Well, sounds like you have a busy life.'

'Well——' she felt bound to defend her boss '—it would have been, but Kyle arranged for me to have a secretary. Anna relieves me of much of the routine grind, otherwise I don't think I could cope.'

'And the pleasure?'

'What?' She stared, embarrassed by the unexpected warmth in her skin, totally thrown by the interjection.

The intense gaze missed nothing. 'You said you were here for business and pleasure. I'm asking about the pleasure.'

'Oh.' Sudden clarity was quickly followed by a sense of relief. 'Oh, that! A friend has just come to Paris to live. We shared a flat for a few months when I first came to Strasbourg and I'm planning to meet up with her again. She's married now, with a baby, so there will be lots to talk about.'

By this time they were collecting their things together, and then—it seemed automatic—they shared a trolley as they walked to the barrier with their luggage.

'I suppose you do have someone coming to pick you up?'

When the forceful dark eyes swept over her, from the top of her gleaming head to the toes of her highly polished black boots, she felt confident, childishly so, that he would find little to criticise. She was wearing tight navy trousers topped by a Cossack-style blouse in a rich peony-coloured silk, with a very English hacking-jacket in heathery checks slung over her shoulders...

He was studying her, while she, with a throb in her stomach as their eyes met, did exactly the same to him. He was the archetypal jet-setting lawyer. She tried to be dismissive and failed miserably. He was the kind of man women of any age would look at twice and then keep on looking. When she had known him all those years ago she had grown used to seeing him in more casual gear, but now he was equally at ease in the dark business suit, snowy shirt and striped tie. Everything about him was immaculate, not a bit like Kyle, who seemed to have a permanently crumpled look...

Suddenly aware that Patrick was still watching her, now with a faintly amused look, she began, without knowing why, to shake her head. Instantly she found herself wondering if he had noticed that she had discarded the riotous hairdo in favour of the sleek look, the heavy swaths of dark hair now held back from her face by two antique silver and tortoiseshell combs which had once belonged to her great-grandmother. But then his question was being repeated, and she felt heat wash over her in an overwhelming wave...

'Sorry. I was dreaming. No, we're expected to make our own way.'

'Then I shall drop you off.' It was a statement rather than a question.

Simply because she was weary—at least, that was how she tried afterwards to justify her weakness—because she was tired, she allowed him to brush her protests, half-hearted in any case, to one side. It wasn't always easy to pick up a taxi and there was no reason why she shouldn't make use of him since he was offering.

A few minutes later, sitting well back in one corner of the rear seat, she tried with a kind of desperate futility to concentrate on the grey peaked hat in front of her, but found that all her attention was on the man by her side.

Paris. The moment she had stepped from the plane at the airport the magic of the place had simply seeped into her bones. Even with him. Or... blindly she looked out on to sun-baked pavements... especially with him. As they drove along the Champs-Elysées, it ought to have been everything that was romantic. At least, she made the correction with firm accuracy, once it would have been. But, right now, sheer unrelieved torture would have been a more apt description. Everywhere she looked, it seemed, her eyes sought out particular pairs of lovers, who had few inhibitions about telling the world just how tender, how delicate, how overwhelming their feelings were...

Oh, this was so idiotic. She closed her eyes tight as they drove past a smiling, entranced young couple. He had been brushing a finger across the outline of her lips and... And causing havoc with the wholly detached feelings of someone he had never even met. Leigh tried to find some amusement in the situation but the struggle with her emotions was intense, and even when she heard his voice she could not bring herself to reply until he had repeated the question.

'What?' Her tone was impatient, verging on the aggressive, and she opened her eyes wide as she turned her head, hoping he might realise that he was intruding into her private space. But then the expression in his eyes held her. She who had once been able to read and sense his every mood was for an instant shocked by the look of stormy anger, something very close to dislike in the dark, searing gaze which raked her. But in a moment it had changed, as if a blank, impassive shutter had been lowered.

Shaken, she tried to warn herself. Be careful. Detachment is what you must show. 'I'm sorry, I was miles away again.' Her voice was admirably calm.

'I was asking about what you've been doing...since...since we last met.'

'I presume you mean since last week.' It was a half-hearted attempt to turn it into a joke.

'You know that's not what I mean.' For a second time she sensed his restrained edginess.

'Well, let me see.' By pretending to consider she regained a little self-confidence. 'I started off doing some research for an MP.' Difficult to resist the word 'tinpot', but why give him the satisfaction of knowing how it had rankled over the years? 'Then I was with an advertising agency for some time—not exactly the career profile I had mapped out when I was slogging for my degree, but there... Anyway, about two years ago I was approached by Kyle to see if I'd be interested in working for him. And of course I was, couldn't resist the challenge, and...well, here I am. Things couldn't have worked out better,' she added triumphantly.

'So... no regrets?'

'None at all.' And even if she had, then this man was the very last one who would hear about them. 'I love the work and Kyle is a very considerate boss—demanding too, but I like that. And, of course, working abroad is a bonus.'

'Of course.' His tone was so dry, so very nearly sarcastic that in spite of herself she swung round to study his face, and was able to see from the lights of passing cars his cynically smiling mouth.

'You sound surprised.' Her sharpness betrayed the anger she felt.

'A little, perhaps.'

'Why? I wonder. Don't most people these days look for at least a spell abroad?'

'I do so agree.' The sarcasm again. 'Only... I thought in your case...' As her brain was trying to latch on to the way his mind was working she was thrown by another question, which at first seemed wholly disconnected. 'How are your parents?' His tone was deceptively casual. 'I meant to ask about them earlier.'

'My par——' Of course, how could she have been so foolish, handing him sticks to beat her with? Her skin burned guiltily, and she turned swiftly aside in an effort to conceal it. 'My parents are fine. My father is still at Great Whencote.' Maybe he wouldn't ask about her mother. Some time later she might let it drop about...

'And your mother too, I presume?' How lightly it was tossed, innocently, as if nothing lay behind his persistence.

'Yes, she's well. Better than she's been for many years. In fact she's in New Zealand right now; she's spending some time out there with her sister.'

'I see.' A simple comment, but his tone implied that he was placing all kinds of interpretations on the information, and nothing, she told herself with silent passion, nothing would induce her to make excuses on her mother's behalf. He wasn't the type to be sympathetic towards other people's weaknesses. Families like the Cavours, so strong and healthy in every way, just wouldn't understand. Her mother was entitled to a long holiday with relatives she hadn't seen for years, and besides, it wasn't that he was interested in her mother; he merely wanted to remind her of her refusal to go to Bangladesh, and she was damned if she would allow herself to be reminded, much less excuse herself or apologise.

Instead she decided that she would attack, and sat quietly trying to compose a pertinent question about Gillian Place without—most certainly without—giving a clue to the corrosive jealousy which had afflicted her for years. But before she could find the right words he was leaning forward, speaking to the chauffeur in French so fluent that it was a moment before she took in what was being said.

'But——' she was breathless with indignation '—there is no need for that.'

'Nonsense.' Even as he spoke they were leaving the main traffic stream, turning into one of the quiet squares and slowing down. 'I'll see you safely inside and——'

'But...' Almost at once she was being helped from the car. 'But I heard you telling the driver that——'

'That's right.' Patrick retrieved her bag from the boot, slammed it shut, waved the driver off and strode across the pavement to the entrance of an apartment block. 'I told him I would walk back. It's only a short distance and I enjoy stretching my legs.'

She found herself ushered through the glass doors, heard the concierge being asked for the key, then she was being guided towards the lift, and all without the slightest reference to her.

'You know——' her irritation was barely controlled '—I am quite capable of asking for my own keys. Even in a foreign language.'

'Of *course* you are.' To her surprise and, rather more unexpectedly, to her pleasure, he gave a tiny shamefaced grin. 'I'm sorry. I'm inclined to be bossy at times, or so my mother tells me.'

'"Overbearing" is the word I would have used.' But at the same time she softened towards him; his attitude had done much to defuse her anger. At one time, the thought fluttered unbidden into her mind, long ago, she would have chosen the word 'masterful', would even, such had been her naïveté, have approved. How simple could one be, for heaven's sake? Now she asked, knowing that she ought to have done so before, as soon as he had mentioned his mother, 'How are things at Loughskerrie?'

'Oh, everything's all right. Lots of changes, of course.' They reached the door of the service flat and he held out the key. 'I won't come in, thank you. But . . .'

Quickly glancing at his face, she saw no sign of mockery, but decided he needed putting in his place. 'I had no intention at all of inviting you.' But it was impossible to control her mouth completely, which was curving, faintly, it was true, but with a distinct suggestion of amusement.

'But,' he continued, as if she hadn't spoken, the dark eyes holding hers in a way that invited her to share memories, with a look which she remembered so well and which she discovered could still threaten havoc, 'there's a lot I could tell you about Loughskerrie and the family—they still speak of you, you know. So I was going to suggest that, if you agree, I could come and pick you up later. We could have dinner—there's a quiet little bistro—and . . . I could bring you up to date . . .'

'Oh . . .' How could she, in spite of all her determination, have let it come to this? She might have guessed what was in his mind, seen the invitation coming. 'Oh, no, thank you. I have plans for this evening and . . .' She shook her head, feeling the dark mass of hair float out, but because her face was so deliberately averted she missed the way his eyes followed its filmy movement, missed, too, the sudden naked pain so swiftly contained in their depths.

'Ah ... Then some other time perhaps.'

'Perhaps,' she agreed, but in a particular tone of contradiction which was unmistakable. 'Oh, and——' she had barely noticed his goodnight, and called after him as he stepped into the lift '—and thank you.' But the doors slammed shut and she was uncertain that he had heard.

The door to the tiny hall was barely closed, and she had hardly taken a step towards the single bedroom she used in Paris, when a sudden rat-a-tat, imperative and impatient, took her hurrying back, cheeks glowing, heart hammering in excited relief and a quite inexplicable anticipation.

'Pa——' The greeting was stifled on her lips. Her sense of disappointment was like a blow when she saw who was standing there. She held open the door. 'Oh, Kyle.' Her voice was flat, weary. 'I didn't expect to see you. I thought you were due on an early flight for Strasbourg.'

'I just wanted to give you this.' He offered her a file which she took without enthusiasm. 'Thought it would help with your meeting tomorrow.'

'Is Anna with you?'

'Mmm. Downstairs in the car. I met Patrick Cavour in the hallway.'

'He gave me a lift from the airport—we were on the same flight from Strasbourg. Just by chance,' she added, to her own vexation.

'Really?' He didn't sound even faintly interested, for which she was thankful and which made her self-conscious excuse doubly redundant. 'Well——' he glanced at his watch '—I must dash or we'll miss our plane, but thanks, Leigh, for sparing Anna for the last few days. It really did make life much easier while I was here.'

'Good.' She looked up from the file she was holding. 'Well, it was a chance for her to come to Paris. She coped with everything?'

'Yes. Marvellously. And, as you say, it's been good experience for her. Well, see you in a few days.'

'What? Oh, yes. Goodbye, Kyle.'

When she was alone in the flat, Leigh walked to the window and stood looking out over rooftops gleaming softly in the light from street-lamps but without seeing them. Thoughts of Kyle, of Anna, of her own reasons for being in Paris at all were totally submerged in an overwhelmingly dismal sense of loss and deprivation which was difficult to explain.

And, annoyingly, those feelings seemed to be centred on the fact that she had been invited out to dinner by a man from her past, an attractive man, most people would agree, but the one man in the world to whom she was no longer susceptible.

So why, in heaven's name, had she refused so precipitately? The query floated into her mind in a despairing kind of way. Here she was, being offered the perfect opportunity to convince herself that her feelings for him were, if not entirely platonic, at least under control, and she had tossed it away, had even given him the impression that any subsequent invitations would be similarly rejected.

He was bound to have picked up the idea that she didn't trust herself in his company; the very notion was humiliating. She ought to have gone with him, made polite, light-hearted conversation, asked all sorts of questions about his family—in short, acted exactly as she would have done with all the other old friends from those days. That would have cemented in his mind the futility of hankering after the past . . . and maybe even in her own mind.

She thrust aside the idea that she needed any convincing, but all the same . . . it would have been nice if she could have rid herself of the load of bitterness and pain which she had carried around with her all these years. She might even have been able to eliminate the baleful significance that Gillian Place's name had assumed in her thoughts. If she had been able to frame a light-hearted question she could have discovered how deeply he had been involved.

Back here, alone in her flat, it was easy to imagine herself with him in the restaurant, when they reached the coffee stage, when her wine glass had been drained and she was feeling mellow and relaxed. She would lean forward, elbows on the table, fingers linked together, supporting her chin, and she would ask, frowning a little, as if the thought had just come into her head, 'And how did that girl—what was her name, now?— she was a nurse, I think, a friend of Debbie . . . Oh, yes.' Her face would clear as the name burned on her mind all at once came to her. 'Gillian Place. How did she fit into the project in Ashala?'

She could imagine no situation in which Patrick Cavour would actually blush, but he would certainly be taken aback; most likely he would look down into his coffee-cup, spend a great deal of time stirring slowly, then he would look up at her. 'So you know about Gillian, do you?'

'Mmm.' She would sip her coffee, press her lips together as she savoured the brew. 'Yes, Debbie told me that you had taken her out to Bangladesh with you. I expect you found her a great asset, a qualified nurse, and doubtless in other ways too.'

Oh... what was the use? Angry with herself, she turned abruptly from the window. There was no way she could remain cool and detached if she were to bring up that name. The mere mention of it to Patrick Cavour and her voice would become all wobbly, and more likely than not she would burst into tears and have to make a blind dash for the ladies' room, returning with some transparent fiction about an allergy which caused her to cough and sneeze at the most inconvenient times.

No, she had made entirely the right decision. She refused to consider any regrets where he was concerned. Her life nowadays was good, and all the time getting better. At this moment all she wanted for complete contentment was a quick shower, a pleasant meal and then an early night with some escapist fiction.

The tears which streaked her cheeks were very soon obliterated in a douche of warm water.

CHAPTER THREE

As she finished dressing, Leigh stood in front of
the mirror swiftly applying make-up, acknowl-
edging that her depression was beginning to lift.
All day she had been feeling down—something
to do with a restless night in a strange bed, and
added to that the stultifying boredom of the
meeting she had had to attend. She must remember to dodge Kyle's suggestions in future.
Even an afternoon window-gazing along some of
the most exciting streets in the world hadn't
managed to eliminate her melancholy.

But now, about to set off on a visit which
promised only pleasure, devoid of the near-
trauma of recent encounters, she felt she might
be on the road to recovery. Besides, it was very
difficult to remain depressed when the mirror was
giving such very encouraging signals, when the
blouse she had picked up in a tiny boutique
looked so good with this favourite skirt.

Holly had implied that it was to be a casual
evening so the tiered cotton skirt would be about
right. The gauzy blouse with ruffled plunging
neckline and full bracelet sleeves ... well, a bit
fancy perhaps, but then she never could resist
those intense midnight shades, which had a
magical effect on her looks as well as her spirits,

and her hair was long enough to twist into the cottage-loaf style which suited her.

Almost satisfied now, she stood back, approving the elegant sway of the skirt, adjusting the wide belt which drew attention to the slender waist. A touch more lipstick to outline the mouth, a tiny spray of flowery scent, and she was ready to meet Paul Santorini III and IV. Just the parcels to pick up—a gorgeous teddy bear with a huge red tartan bow, pralines for chocaholic Holly and whisky for Paul, of whose preferences she was entirely ignorant. She walked downstairs just as her cab pulled up in front of the apartment block.

'Doesn't she look glamorous?' Having introduced her husband and her best friend, and expressed delight over the gifts, Holly swept them both in front of her and into the long, elegant salon.

'She does.' Offering a tray with glasses of chilled wine, Paul exchanged an amused glance with Leigh. 'I'm very impressed.'

'Did I describe her properly?' Then, without waiting for a reply, 'She hasn't changed a bit.'

'I wonder if you described me properly to Leigh?' her husband teased. 'And, come to that, does she think you've changed much?'

'Oh, me?' Holly shrugged ruefully. 'I bet all she notices is that I've put on about twenty pounds. That,' she sighed, 'is what being blissfully happy and having a baby does for you.'

'I can't entirely agree with you there.' Paul was perfectly serious. 'I've had a baby too, wouldn't dare to be less than blissfully happy, and haven't gained an ounce.'

'Idiot.' His wife threw a cushion at him and missed. 'People who won't put on weight make me sick. But, speaking of babies...I'm sure Leigh is dying to see our little wonder.'

'I thought you'd never mention it.' Leigh spoke with more tact than truth and a moment later she was being led across the hall and into the nursery.

'We'll just peep at him, but you're sure to see him later because he always wakes up about ten.'

When they were leaning over the cot and Leigh had made all the appropriately admiring comments she said softly, at the same time putting out a finger to touch the downy, incredibly soft cheek, 'I'm glad you're so happy, Holly.'

After a pause her friend agreed. 'So happy. And so lucky, I just can't believe it. After what happened in Strasbourg...' She referred to a disastrous affair she had had two years earlier. 'That was all such a waste of time.'

'Yes, you're lucky to have met a man like Paul, and——' Leigh glanced round the beautifully appointed nursery '—to have such a lovely home.'

'Mmm, we were lucky to find it. It's a fairly international block—several Americans, which suits Paul, and a general mix of Europeans.' From the hall they heard the doorbell ring, the faint sound of feet walking on thick carpet, followed by a door opening. 'As a matter of fact, we've asked one of our neighbours to join us for supper—that'll be him arriving now. Paul knew him slightly before... We'll go now. As I said,

Pauli will be sure to wake before you go.' Switching off the light, Holly guided her guest back towards the salon, to the murmur of voices, the chink of glasses. Then a sudden low laugh brought Leigh to a halt.

'Come on, love.' Smiling, Holly stood there, hand on the doorknob. 'Don't say you're shy.'

'Of course not.' But she had a shivery sensation down her backbone. Nothing she could identify, but a feeling of apprehension . . .

'Then come and meet Patrick; I know you'll like each other.'

Somehow, in spite of legs like jelly, Leigh forced herself forward and through the door, guessing from the expression on his face that the meeting was as unexpected for Patrick as it was for her. It was difficult to discern whether it was as unwelcome—he had the lawyer's habit of impassivity when it suited—but at least he carried it off with a convincing degree of casual surprise.

'Leigh.' There was a fraught second before he raised his glass in her direction. 'I had no idea we were to meet up again so soon.'

'No.' Her mouth twisted into what she hoped would pass for a smile. 'Nor I.' The colour which had drained from her face now began to return as she spoke to Holly. 'We travelled together from Strasbourg yesterday.'

'How amazing.' For some reason their hostess seemed disappointed. 'You actually know each other.'

'Yes. I had to go to Strasbourg last week and we met there.' At least he was as keen to play down the length of their acquaintance as Leigh was. 'And by chance we found ourselves on the same flight.'

'I've just been inspecting Paul Santorini IV.' It seemed vital to change the subject, so Leigh smiled at the parents. 'He's a gorgeous child, and I'm inclined to agree with all those ecstatic descriptions.'

'Well, my wife does tend to go over the top, so you must excuse her.' Smiling down at her, Paul put an arm about Holly's waist. 'But now dare I ask when you are going to feed us? I'm starving, and I suspect Leigh and Patrick are too.'

'It's all ready. So if you'll all come through we can start to eat.'

Although Leigh was seated opposite Patrick, the very last position she would have chosen, the two men were having a discussion about cars and she was able at first to ignore him. But that did not mean she was unaware. Every nerve in her body, it seemed, was acutely sensitive. As she spoke to Holly, looked at Holly, it was Patrick she was seeing: light tweed jacket, which, with his hostess's permission, he had taken off and slung over the back of his chair, jade silk shirt with a slightly exotic pink tie, dark trousers. Every inch the off-duty professional man, she thought with a touch of sourness.

Then he caught her whole attention with that unconscious, heart-melting gesture she remembered so well: a hand going up to sweep back that persistently uncontrolled lock of hair and—— She drew a deep, embarrassed breath when she realised he was looking at her—in fact they all were, obviously waiting for some comment.

'I think Leigh would say she's perfectly happy where she is; at least, I got that impression when we spoke on the plane.' Patrick was helping her out, covering up. She supposed she ought to be grateful, not resentful. 'She has no thoughts of changing jobs for the time being.' An inclination of his head offered a clue and Leigh turned to Paul with a smile. 'I think you're being head-hunted.'

'You're not offering me a job, Paul?'

'No, I wouldn't dare, in view of what Holly has said about your relationship with your boss, but I simply wondered... Most people enjoy a change of scene from time to time, especially people who are free to move around without family commitments.'

'Well——' this was too good a chance to miss '—at one time I did have problems, and had to stay in the UK, but now things are easier. I can please myself but, even so, I'm not thinking of a move in the near future. I can't imagine any job being more attractive than the one I have at present, hopping back and forward between Paris and Strasbourg. And it's so easy to go to other countries—the centre of Europe, you might say.'

'Talking about exciting jobs...' Holly paused as she served pudding '...I don't suppose you know—or maybe you do!' She gave a tiny laugh. 'After all, I had no idea that you and Patrick knew each other... Anyway, did you hear that at one time Patrick worked for one of the major relief agencies? Where was it again, Patrick? India somewhere?'

'Mmm. At least, in Bangladesh. A place called Ashala.' As he spoke he looked directly across at Leigh, doubtless noticing the increased colour in her cheeks, the determined way she was avoiding his gaze. 'I don't suppose you'll have heard of it, Leigh.'

'Mmm. *I* certainly haven't.' Holly luckily didn't notice the look of irritation which passed from one of her guests to the other, but then she asked, '*Have* you, Leigh?'

'What?' Startled, she turned her eyes on her hostess. 'Sorry, Holly...?'

'Have you heard of this place Patrick mentioned? Ashala? In Bangladesh?' she added helpfully.

'It sounds...a bit familiar.' Defiantly she held his gaze. 'But *do* tell us about it,' she encouraged with a synthetic smile. 'I'm sure we're all...very interested.'

'As a matter of fact——' and now Holly and Paul had ceased to exist; there was just the two of them, each challenging the other in turn '—it's got to have been the most worthwhile experience of my life. You know how it is—you regret so much that seemed important for a little while. And it's not simply for the little you're able to put in yourself, it's seeing how people cope every day, and in circumstances impossible to imagine unless you've had the experience—how they deal with everyday hazards——' He broke off, picked up his spoon and ate some chocolate mousse.

'I'd been there just a few weeks when there were tremendous storms; a flash-flood washed all their pathetic possessions away, but the next day the waters had gone down and they began getting things together again. No complaining, no whingeing because there was no time, and anyway, life for them is a constant battle with nature.'

For just a moment Leigh was seeing him stripped to the waist, thigh-deep in swirling muddy water, trying to hold the roof on a rickety attap hut... Then, sensing his attention, she came out of her reverie, turning in relief as Holly spoke again.

'It's the kind of thing I wish I had done when I first left college. It's too late once you're married and have children, but how I wish I'd had the opportunity. I do admire you, Patrick, for having had the drive to do it.' She had no idea how much pain she was inflicting.

All Patrick's charm was directed towards his hostess as he touched his mouth with a napkin. 'Now don't start polishing my halo. That's the last thing I want or deserve. In fact all of us who were there agree on one thing—that we were the ones who gained.'

'All of you...' Leigh's voice was a little shrill, all to do with her confused feelings—first that vision of him, elemental and arousing, then the cold douche as he repeated the words she had spent years regretting. She swallowed, began again. 'How many of you were on that particular project?'

'Including the medical staff——' again his attention was on her face '—about a dozen. Plus a few who turned up from time to time to spend a few weeks with us, usually students in the long vacations.'

'I see...' She was playing for time, trying to find a casual way of introducing Gillian Place's name. It would be so satisfying to let him know that she had heard... But her voice took on a waspish tone as she switched tack. 'I would have thought there might be difficulties in putting in such a large number...'

'Oh?' One dark eyebrow was raised questioningly. His tone was bland but there was little doubt that he knew she was being difficult.

'Yes.' Contrarily Leigh was now regretting becoming involved; she would hate Holly and Paul to imagine that she had such a sour view of life that even the best of motives were suspect—she didn't want even *him* to see her in that light— but now she had embarked... 'So many Westerners, all with high standards of living. Isn't it quite difficult arranging for supplies to be ferried in for large groups?'

'That, in fact, was no problem.' If she had rubbed him up the wrong way he wasn't showing it. 'The organisation we belonged to has a rule: all fieldworkers live at the same level as the natives. Of course that wouldn't apply in famine conditions—little point in dropping people in to swell the numbers starving—but where the subsistence level is low everyone has to accept the local standards. Naturally, that isn't to say that if someone became seriously ill he wouldn't be ferried out, but no...we lived with the locals, and as a result most of us lost the odd half-stone while we were there...'

'I see.' Leigh was trying very hard not to blush; she sensed she was failing but she did manage to produce a smile for her host and hostess. She just hoped it wasn't too apologetic. 'Well, that would seem to be the only sensible way to operate in the circumstances.'

A brief smile aimed at the other two faded as Patrick stared across the table at Leigh. 'But the first shock of going there is when you arrive. You're simply unprepared for the sheer beauty of the place. Your mind has been programmed for the dirt and dust associated with grinding poverty, but we came to Ashala in the early evening when the sun was setting. There was a golden haze over the river, an air of such peace and tranquillity that I wondered what we were doing there. It seemed so much like the spot we'd all love to escape to.'

Even the cold look in his eyes could not damp down the wave of intense melancholy and regret that swept through Leigh at the thought that she might have gone with him, seen life through such different eyes and—— He was continuing.

'But then, of course, things change.' Again his expression was adding to the words, accusing her. 'Nature takes a hand, like the flood I just mentioned...'

Paul was toying with his glass. 'That must have been terrifying.'

'Strangely enough, it happened so quickly you had no time to think. First of all the people tried to get the children away to higher ground—the villages tend to lie along the riverbanks—then they came back to try to save what they could. They're so hard-working, and certainly don't deserve the opinion some of us have——' and now his look was even more critical '—that they ought to do more to help themselves. That is precisely what they do, and in the long term they are the ones who will win the battle against poverty and disease. Certainly it won't be won by the pathetic hand-outs they get from the West.' His smile was directed at his hostess, and was charming and self-mocking. 'Here ends the lesson.'

'Thank you for telling us about it, Patrick. It must have been a worthwhile experience in every way.'

'Well, as I said, it sorts out the priorities. One's whole perspective changes. All the minor things which were once so important seem to drift away, and with luck——' though he was no longer looking at her Leigh had little doubt that this was a personal attack '—none of them will ever be so important again.'

She was so involved with her own raised emotions, so highly sensitised by everything he had said, that for a moment Leigh didn't realise they were being invited through to the salon. There Holly began to pour coffee, while urging her husband to refill glasses.

'As I said before——' she handed a cup to Leigh while speaking to Patrick '—I feel quite desperate that I didn't do something along those lines years ago. And of course——' here she wrinkled her brow with the effort of remembering '—you did something along those lines too, didn't you, Leigh?'

'I did?' Feeling colour rising in her cheeks and still more conscious of those dark eyes trained to miss nothing, Leigh stared at her hostess in an attempt to convey total discouragement. 'No, of course not...'

But Holly, involved with coffee and pressing Patrick to take cream, was oblivious. 'Yes, you did.' She spared a quick glance towards her husband. 'Drinks coming, darling? Of course you did, love.' She returned to her theme. 'Remember that first Christmas when we were all going skiing, but you wouldn't because you were involved with Crisis at Christmas? At St Martin-in-the-Fields,' she explained to Patrick who, Leigh could see without looking at him, was wearing his brooding Heathcliff expression.

'That was nothing.' Paul's offer of a liqueur was a relief. 'No, not for me, Paul.' She was normally abstemious, rarely drank more than two glasses of wine, rarely wanted more. 'The wines were delicious, but I've had enough.'

'And I seem to remember——' Holly could be exasperatingly tenacious when she chose '—you drove a load of supplies to Romania.'

'Just a tiny one.' Even to herself she had never analysed her reasons for doing those things, but

certainly they had had nothing to do with...
anyone else...

She became aware that Paul was trying to persuade her to change her mind. 'It *is* a special occasion, after all—you and Holly meeting up like
this when you were such friends before...'

'Go on.' Holly joined her husband. 'Besides,
I... at least, Paul and I... have a great favour to
ask, and we want to try to get you into a re-
ceptive mood.'

'We-ell.' For a moment she hesitated, and then
gave way. 'Just a very little.' She watched Paul
splash some of the amber liquid into a large glass,
took it and placed it on the nearby table. 'You
said something about a special favour...'

'Yes, a very special one.' Holly had always had
the inclination to make mysteries from the sim-
plest events.

'Then if it's at all possible I'll be happy to do
what I can.' Leigh had a sinking feeling that she
might be invited to act as nanny while the parents
took themselves off for a weekend break. Naturally she would have to agree, so long as
everyone understood that she knew nothing about
infants. 'And I don't need alcohol to persuade
me. At least——' her eyes widened in a parody
of apprehension '—I *hope* it isn't one of those
promises—the kind extracted when one's normal
common sense has gone out the window?'

Paul laughed. 'It might be best described as a
lifetime's commitment.' But it was obvious he
was teasing.

'Oh, *dear*, it's beginning to sound quite threatening.' And Leigh mopped her forehead, still laughing at herself but still completely puzzled.

'Paul and I——' Holly slipped a hand into her husband's '—would be thrilled if you would agree to be Pauli's godmother.'

'G-godmother.' The idea was so surprising that her mind went blank for a second, then her face flushed with pleasure.

'Please say you will,' Holly persuaded. 'The christening is in two weeks' time, right here in Paris.'

'Well, of course.' Conscious of Patrick's close attention, as well as the colour coming and going in her cheeks, she felt awkward and conspicuous. 'I would be flattered and delighted.'

'So you agree?' Holly's expression was total pleasure. 'Oh, thank you, Leigh. There's no one else I wanted to ask. I'm so grateful to you both, in fact. Patrick,' she explained, 'is to be one of the godfathers.'

And when Leigh's startled glance transferred to Patrick's face she could tell from his raised eyebrow just how much sardonic amusement he was deriving from her discomfiture.

'Oh, and I shall let you know all about timings in a day or two. It's such a pity you're going to be so busy while you're in Paris.'

Before long, when, in spite of all Holly's promises, the baby showed no sign of waking, Leigh, suddenly exhausted and very nearly as dejected as she had been earlier, decided it was time to go, and would not be persuaded otherwise.

'It *is* getting late.' Patrick glanced at his watch and got up. 'I'd better go too. I'm sure you two are ready for bed—I just hope that Pauli will realise that as well.' Forestalling Leigh, who was about to ask if she could ring for a cab, he added, 'I can see Leigh safely into a cab. It's easier to pick one up on the corner than to ring.'

It seemed boorish to object so she smiled as goodnights were said and promises repeated, but when she and Patrick were walking to the lift she allowed her irritation to simmer. He was equally silent, standing with his jacket looped over his shoulder, till a sudden, unexpected spatter of rain against the window made them glance round.

'Hmm. A bit of a squall.' As they stepped inside the lift his attention was all on her, from the top of her head to her slender feet in strappy impractical sandals. 'And you...' his voice had softened, though his eyes were dark and sombre '...you are scarcely dressed for stormy weather.'

All at once she was having trouble with her breathing; her heart was hammering so insistently against her chest, it seemed impossible that he wouldn't hear. And standing so close, so close that she was aware of the heat emanating from his body, she was forced to press her fingernails into the palms of her hands to stop them from reaching out. The desire was so strong, near irresistible, and... the lift was stopping.

'But...' There was more than a hint of desperation in her manner as her eyes searched the control panel. 'But we're not at ground level.'

'No, this is my floor. I can pick up an umbrella.' As if nature was on his side a sudden gust swirled about the building; she could have sworn it moved, but... 'I can even lend you a raincoat, if that would help.'

Her will was shot to pieces, which would explain why she followed him along the corridor, watched him slip the key into the lock then stand aside for her to go first, which she did meekly.

How warm and peaceful it felt—and safe. Thick carpets cushioned their feet, table-lamps with pink shades cast a soft glow; she had an impression of a few water-colours on the walls and there was even music, faint, disturbing, sensuous and utterly distracting—Rachmaninov, brushing at her nerve-endings as raw silk might till she felt... She couldn't even have explained what she felt, except that her blood was afire, and she was thinking he had the most beautiful mouth ever seen on...

'Leigh.' It was the merest sigh in her ears; she would not even have said he had spoken, though her eyes, wide and luminous, searched his face, then, not answering, she swayed towards him.

There was this soft, susurrant sound in her throat, pain mixed with pleasure, and her eyelids drifted closed, allowing her imagination to run riot. She was drowning in the remembered sensation of fingertips moving over warm, smooth skin. It hadn't died, that first intoxicating wonder that anything so frankly male should be so smooth, so... so utterly beguiling. And then a flicker of shadowy eyelids and she could confirm that this was no dream. If she wanted, all she had to do was reach out, stroke . . .

'Leigh.' Now there was no doubt. Who else had ever used her name with that throbbing, *wondering* intensity? Who else? She shivered a little as the hands traversed the length of her arms, circled the delicate wrists, raised her palms, kissed each in turn. Then—and how often they had exclaimed at the perfection of this—he inclined her body into the accommodating curve of his.

And his mouth . . . An aching sob escaped her lips as his brushed them once or twice, then she tried briefly, hopelessly, to snatch at her emotions, which were spiralling out of control. Then, failing, she surrendered completely, caught his head between her palms, stopping the unbearable teasing movements, holding him there as slowly, slowly, she allowed her lips to part, offering the access which it was now impossible to refuse.

'Leigh?' Now his breathing was fast, exciting, and the dark eyes repeated the question so apparent in the way he spoke her name. And there was a tiny frown, a faint pulling together of eyebrows, a fierce intensity about him, as if he was determined to brand her image on to his psyche.

And she, light-years from her carefully nurtured discretion, replied with one word—his name, uttered on a note of sighing longing, her violet eyes hazy and signalling the total submission which was all that was in her mind. 'Patrick.' And she laid her head against his chest.

A split-second passed, as if time had been arrested, then, with no risk of misunderstanding, he swept her up and strode towards one of the doors, which was shouldered open. Only as they reached the bedside did he begin to release her, allowing her feet almost to touch the floor, suspended in intimate contact with his body.

'You're sure?' He spoke with exquisite concern and tenderness but she couldn't reply, not with one hand brushing down her cheek, the other circling her throat—but then there was no need. All that was needed she did, reaching out with trembling impatient fingers to unfasten the buttons of his shirt, to trail through that scatter of curling black hair, to pick up in the sensitive tips the throbbing of his pulses which seemed such an echo of her own. Then, at last, she leaned forward to press the softness of her cheek against the warm flesh, to explore its contours with her mouth.

His hands travelled the length of her spine, fingers dealing swiftly with awkward clips and fastenings, and she felt herself succumbing completely to a blur of pleasure as the delicate blouse was eased from her shoulders. She moaned as their bodies moved together in a contact which was building up her fevered excitement. She had forgotten... Eyes half closed, she tried for a split-second to be detached. She had forgotten, or more likely she had deliberately banished from her memory, the sheer magic of *this* activity with *this* man. Even the most abandoned dream could never begin to reach the peak of pure sensation she was experiencing now. All she wanted was for him to... 'Patrick.' The sigh was a blatant entreaty.

'Leigh.' His reply was a promise as the last restrictive garments fell to the floor and he lifted her up, placing her on the bed, gazing down for a moment before joining her there. 'You can have no idea...'

But words faded, the world faded; all senses were drifting, drowning on a tide of sheer delight, while the notes of the romantic Russian prelude were being branded on two souls.

CHAPTER FOUR

WHEN she woke in the dimness of the strange bedroom, stark naked and barely covered with a sheet, Leigh's mind went blank, eyes moving with feverish panic about the walls as she tried to identify the room. Then, as signals in her brain began to click, she drew in one sudden fearful breath, lay perfectly still for a moment, before slowly turning her head on the pillow, biting back a cry of denial directed towards the powerful predator. Just then Patrick stirred, one dark hand reaching out towards her before falling back, fingers curving within inches of her arm.

Scarcely breathing, she lay there, watching the even rise and fall of the broad chest, a potent surge low in her stomach reminding her of the delicious sensation of touch, how it had given him such pleasure. His throaty sounds of delight were still echoing in her brain, and a scalding heat on her skin emphasised her admission that the reverse was equally true. Each time his fingers had skimmed, touched, tantalised, she had cried aloud at the intensity of it, arching against him in a shameless search for fulfilment.

And that was what she had attained. He had made sure of it for her, though that had been unnecessary the first time—that fierce instantaneous joining had left no time for the coaxing languorous wonder which had come later, taking her to such peaks of glorious moaning delight. Even thinking of it now in the chill light of dawn made her feel weak and shivery, and she brought one hand up in a slow, exploratory sweep of her body in a desire to capture those elusive sensations.

Anger stabbed unexpectedly. Not that it should have happened, and she would never be able to explain why it had. Such behaviour was so entirely out of character. Leaving the security of Holly's flat upstairs, she had been totally in control of her actions; she might even have felt slightly irritated that she had been in some clever way coerced into a situation which would involve her yet again with the man she was so anxious to avoid, slightly resentful of the matchmaking plans she suspected her friend had been brewing.

But quite apart from that she'd had no suspicion of how vulnerable she was. She had been perfectly confident of walking into his hall to pick up an umbrella, walking out and along to the taxi-rank and back to the company flat. But, instead, a touch of his hand and she had been swept into the powerful whirlpool of emotions that he had always been able to produce... A quizzically raised eyebrow, a finger-touch on her inner wrist or at the nape of her neck and...

She was mortified, filled with self-disgust. So many years of abstinence—what on earth could have possessed her? She brushed angrily at a tear. Probably the music; she had always been a sucker for that particular piece of Rachmaninov...

Possibly... her brain was whirling... the sensual assault had lowered her resistance and...

It was all so *contrived*. That conclusion came to her in a rush. It was so sordid. He must have known she was to be the guest at Holly's last night—they must have mentioned her name, or even a few hints would have been enough for him to reach the right answer. So the scene had been carefully set, the trap baited, and she... she had fallen in. Ugh.

With one lithe, graceful movement, she got up, moving carefully to collect her scattered clothes. She took a last look around to check that she had forgotten nothing—the very notion of him pursuing her with some intimate item of clothing... A final lingering look towards the bed, her primitive instinct to go back emphasising the ease and pleasure of abandoned principles, and she was in the hall, searching for the bathroom, quickly pulling on the clothes she had liked so much just a short time ago. Then, lastly, she scribbled a note and left it in a prominent position.

So it was that, just minutes after waking, she was alighting from a cab outside her block, having asked the driver to return in an hour to take her to the opposite side of the city for her first appointment.

And it wasn't until she was showered and dressed, impeccably if a little severely, hanging on like grim death as the driver moved from one fast-moving lane of traffic to the other, that she felt comparatively safe from the immediate threat of an irate Irishman.

Never, she told herself as they screeched round the Place de la République, never had she felt so low. Not even when Patrick had gone off to Bangladesh with Gillian Place. That name, the one that had burned in her heart for years, seemed to make her behaviour last night even more irrational.

For Holly had hinted, during one of the brief periods when Leigh had helped clear things away from the table, that she knew Patrick had had a great sorrow in his life and that she was trusting that Leigh might help take his mind off it. 'Something,' she had mouthed almost silently, as they had crossed the hall with trays of dessert, 'that happened when he was abroad, with his aid project.'

Which could mean only one thing, Leigh decided. He and Gillian Place. Something had gone wrong and he had never got over it. And her stupid weakness last night had been ... just inexcusable.

Afterwards, she remembered very little of the day, though she had copious notes from her appointments, and among them a little card with the name of a captain in the Royal Navy. It took her three days to recall the sandy-haired man whose invitation to dinner she had parried with such graceful detachment that he had insisted on giving her his hotel number in case she should find herself unexpectedly free.

In the early evening, as she was driven back across the city, she sat with her eyes closed and found herself unable to switch off the complete replay of those intimate hours spent in Patrick's bed. She was even filled with tortured regret when she remembered that arm outstretched towards her in the dawn. Her body was suddenly urgent for warm, loving flesh, burning for the tender early-morning joy in which laughter had always played a part. Perhaps she had been wrong to...

But no. Deliberately she opened her eyes, as if sheer concentration might clear her mind of so many treacherous ideas. And yet... was it treachery to admit that they had matched as well as they ever did? Better, she admitted with dismal honesty, for last night they had reached glorious heights which even her most abandoned dreams had not prepared her for. And quite naturally that led her to a desperate realisation, one which offered bleak proof, if that were needed. The truth was that one of them was obviously much more experienced, whereas the other... She was the one who had gone through the trauma and loneliness, while he...

Well, she was a fool. A salutary conclusion for an intelligent woman of twenty-five to reach. A fool to have denied herself the comfort of casual relationships taken so much for granted by her contemporaries.

Ah, well—she gave a tiny, bitter smile at her own naïveté—one lived and learned. And in the meantime... With a sudden change of attitude she leaned forward and asked to be dropped off at the little delicatessen close to her flat. She would pick up something to eat, watch television for an hour and then have an early night. She had often found that a cure for...oh, for all kinds of things.

Half an hour later, she leaned back on the door of the flat with a feeling of relief, went to the kitchen to drop off the baguette and slice of pâté, switched on the kettle for coffee, kicked off her shoes and turned to cross to her bedroom.

The sudden and loud rat-a-tat at the door made her jump, and at the same time she felt her heart hammering loudly against her ribs, which was utterly ridiculous and out of character, and in any case he wouldn't have the... It was most likely Anna, except that of course she was in... Reaching the door, she opened it quickly, and stood there as if turned to stone. But of *course*. Who else?

'Leigh.' At that moment she didn't notice the air of strain about him, but later it occurred to her that he was rather pale. Since she showed no sign of moving he asked, rather tentatively for a man as positive as Patrick Cavour, 'May I come in?'

'Yes, of course.' A sudden chill on her skin had given way to burning heat, but it was subsiding a little as she stood aside, allowing him to pass into the small hall where he stood watching while she struggled to retain some dignity as she slipped her feet back into her shoes. Then, with a wave of her hand, she indicated the sitting-room and followed him. The pain was back in her chest—sharp, overwhelming. It took all the courage she could muster to face him with an appearance of calm. 'This is a surprise. I've just this minute come in.'

'I know that. I've been sitting in a corner of the landing waiting for you.'

'You've been what?' Hard to say why this should be such an unpleasant surprise to her.

'I think you heard.' They glared at each other for a moment.

'Then you had no right. None whatsoever. I would have thought——'

'You would have thought what?' Now, with the light from the overhead lamp directly on his face, she could see that he was angry; there was a tightness about his mouth and his tone was short to the point of rudeness. 'That I would take this——' reaching into an inner pocket of his jacket, he produced a sheet of paper which she instantly recognised and waved it in front of her '—my dismissal, like... like a whipped cur? Is that what you'd have thought?'

'N-no.' Inwardly shaking, still she managed a casual shrug. 'I thought you would agree with what I wrote, that you'd see last night for what it was—a pleasant if impulsive interlude.' She had a sudden desperate desire to escape. 'Would you like some coffee? I was just going to make——'

'No.' His voice was dangerously quiet, controlled, but only just, she suspected. 'I would not like some coffee, damn it. If I wanted coffee——' now there was no effort to control his bitterness '—I would have gone to the café on the corner.'

When they glared at each other it was difficult to judge who was angrier—she because he had dared to remind her of the scene on the landing that first night, he for different, more complex reasons. What was undeniable was that both were giving off sparks which were very nearly flammable.

'I'm here,' he said through clenched teeth, 'to find out your excuse for baling out in that particularly offensive way.'

'My reason,' she spat back, 'not my excuse but my reason, is in that letter you're waving about. I think it was perfectly clear.'

'Oh, it was clear. Short and to the point.' Holding it up, he read mockingly, '"Sorry about last night, Patrick."' He took a moment out to flick a glance in her direction, one that doubtless drew conclusions from her burning cheeks. But at least, she comforted herself, the glitter of tears would be hidden beneath her eyelids. He went on, '"An awful mistake."' A pause for emphasis. '"I'm sure you'll agree it's best for me to make myself scarce, save a great deal of embarrassment all round. See you one of these days."'

Another brief silence gave her time to understand at least some of his anger; it did sound awfully like a dismissal, which no man like Patrick Cavour would enjoy...

'Yes, as you say, your message was perfectly clear. Except I don't believe a word of it.' A longer, more expectant silence followed, one which she had no intention of breaking, so he was forced to speak again, and this time she detected a slight softening of his manner. She had to guard against the tiny responsive shivers at the base of her spine. 'I'd much rather you told me the truth, Leigh.'

'No.' She was worried about her reactions, panicky, and afraid of emotions which swung so wildly from one extreme to another. 'No, you wouldn't.' A hand went up to rake the silky hair back from her forehead. 'I promise you.' And she felt confident enough to look him straight in the eye.

Another prolonged silence. Behind the impassive expression she could imagine the keen brain working, picking up clues, weighing the evidence. The one indication of his emotional involvement was the hurried rise and fall of his chest. His pride, she guessed, must have been severely dented, and——

'Tell me why you ran away, Leigh.'

'I don't accept that I ran away... I *left* because——' she bit fiercely at her lower lip '—because I was ashamed.' Tears sparkled blatantly now on her long lashes. 'It's as simple as that.'

'Ashamed?' Clearly it was not what he had expected to hear, any more than she had planned to say it, and her mind raced madly in search of the next logical step... 'But why, in heaven's name? Why?'

'Oh, Patrick.' How she managed to speak his name in that particular tone—amused condescension with a touch of impatience—she couldn't explain, but she had found the perfect cover for her tortured emotions. 'I wonder if you'll believe me if I say I've never been promiscuous?' The word very nearly stuck in her throat. 'I've always had just one relationship at a time, and I felt ... ashamed at what happened last night. It was so unfair.' Even to her own ears the stream of lies sounded utterly genuine and convincing. 'To you, to me—oh, to all of us, really...'

The silence now seemed endless, and his voice, when at last he spoke, was flat, emotionless. 'Ashamed?'

'I told you, didn't I, that you wouldn't like it?'

'And——' the sneer in his voice made her shake with self-disgust '—who is he, this invisible lover who mustn't be betrayed?'

'That is a question you have no right to ask. I wouldn't dream of asking about your——' She glared, bit her lip, unwilling to be too exact in her comments, even though there was one name she longed to throw at him.

'Damn you.' Turning away in obvious fury, he swung back just as she was allowing her misery to show. He took a step closer, searching her features as she fought for composure. 'I wonder if it has occurred to you at all, Leigh——' all at once, he was remarkably detached, cool in a way that only increased her misery '—that there is a chance——' his words were slow in coming, as if each one was being carefully weighed, as if he was performing an unpleasant duty which was none the less affording him some sadistic pleasure '—I would have thought, that you might be pregnant...?'

Her eyes widened in shock as he forced her to recognise the fear that she had spent the entire day trying to chase from her mind, one she wouldn't admit to... 'No.' Her clenched fist came out and hit the table; her tears were almost uncontrollable. 'No!' she repeated, with still more defiant energy.

He continued where he had left off, as if she hadn't spoken. 'If you were to find that you were carrying my child, I would expect—no, more than that, I would demand—that you tell me.'

There was a struggle then; she had to wait for composure so that she could find a calm voice. 'The possibility does not exist—you must just take my word for that. No matter what your opinion of me, I'm not so stupid, so irresponsible...'

'No? Well, take it from me, Leigh, I have strong opinions about certain things, and I would never collude with you in getting rid of——'

'Then maybe...' She was in such emotional distress now that she was barely aware of what she was saying. 'Maybe you should have considered these things before. Then there would have been no need for you to rush across Paris making threats...'

'Was that what I was doing?' He spoke with such weary regret that she was instantly stabbed with remorse. 'It wasn't at all what I meant, but of course...you're entirely right. Before the event was the time to be aware of possible consequences, only...like you, Leigh, but for entirely different reasons...I hadn't meant it to happen. No matter what my inclination, it was enough for the moment...'

'You hadn't meant it to happen!' Anger and misery brought the burst of accusation which would doubtless have been better repressed. 'How can you expect me to believe that?'

Frowning, looking at her intently, he nodded slowly. 'Maybe because it's the truth. Simple as that.'

'You must take me for a fool.' Biting furiously at her lip, she whirled away, staring through the window, with its panoramic view of roofs and trees, but seeing nothing. 'A complete fool.' Shivering, she wrapped her arms about herself and turned, about to face him with her angry accusation.

'No.' His calmness was an insult, when it must have been apparent to him that she was suffering, that he was the source of her suffering. 'I've always known you to be a highly intelligent, rational woman, not a fool...'

'A fool where——' How close she had come to making the fatal error of saying 'you'. She managed just in time to change it to, 'Where men are concerned.' In the present circumstances that still wasn't particularly clever.

'Ah!' To her ears the single exclamation was an acceptance of her supposed lifestyle, but before she could react he continued, 'You still haven't explained what you were hinting at. There was, unless I'm wildly misinterpreting, the suggestion that I had planned——'

'And of course you didn't.' Sarcasm could be so very satisfying, and though it was a pity that it had come to the stage of trading insults there was a certain relief in letting him know how clearly, even if it was retrospectively, she had seen through his plotting.

If she hadn't been so completely overwhelmed by her emotions, so totally dominated by her sensual yearnings, last night need never have happened. She would have summed up the situation the moment her foot stepped on to his luxurious carpet, the instant her ears were assaulted—or insidiously caressed might be a better description—by that erotic music. Even now she could hardly believe she had been so gullible.

'All those soft lights.' It was difficult to subdue her urge to spit the words out at him. 'So much sweet music.' She managed a faint smile, an amused lift of an eyebrow. 'Rachmaninov, am I not right? Are you telling me they were all mere coincidence?'

The expression on his face was inscrutable and somehow deeply wounding. 'What a devious little mind you have.' He gave a short, contemptuous laugh. 'Have you changed so much, I wonder?' He paused; she listened to the violent beating of her heart. 'Or is it merely my memory of you...?' Then he said, more briskly, 'You still haven't explained how I was supposed to know who was going to be there, or is that irrelevant? Was I so crazed, do you suppose, that I might have pounced on whoever turned up?'

'Holly could easily have mentioned my name.'

'She could have, but she didn't. In fact I knew nothing of the invitation until I got home and found the message on the machine, and believe it or not my first instinct was to refuse, since I had a pile of work to catch up on. Come to think of it, it seems a great pity that I didn't stick to my original inclination—don't you agree? Oh, and by the way, the lights, the sweet music—that's another thing you got all wrong. The flats have a series of security devices; one of them switches things off and on at irregular intervals. But you are right on one thing: it was Rachmaninov. Not my choice, in fact, but one of the rather sentimental pieces which tend to appeal to the electronic companies.'

They stood there looking at each other for a long time, then he turned away with a sigh.

'Anyway, to go back to something that you said some time ago, you're probably right on that too—I ought not to have come rushing over here raising Cain. Especially, I ought not to have asked impertinent questions about your private life, and for that I ask your forgiveness. Now the only thing left is for me to go.' He reached the hall and turned. 'But Leigh——' the eyes searching her face were so intense and probing that his next words should not have been surprising '—that girl I once mentioned to you—I'm beginning to wonder if she ever existed.'

When the door had closed behind him, she stood for a while staring blankly at the smooth pale wood, remembering only his final words, the ones that had reached down into the core of her being, searing, wounding. You might have thought that he too... that he had suffered through the years of separation, though she knew he could never have endured as she had.

But, possibly for the first time, she admitted a tiny doubt about her own position. If she had been less determined to protect her own pride, if she had been less abrasive, less resolved to hide her own loneliness, then—who could say?—they might have ended up as friends, at least.

Except, she reminded herself, before she could go far along that regretful road, she could never forgive the betrayal with Gillian Place. But, in spite of everything, some of the sting had gone even from that. It was impossible to whip up the anger and indignation which had once come so easily, and which had probably hurt her more than anything else.

And, in any case, wasn't that what love came down to in the end? Certainly it was what many people believed. Everyone had human weaknesses, relied on those who truly loved them to pardon. To forgive.

And was it possible that she had just thrown away the perfect opportunity to show how forgiving she could be? The treacherous thought was difficult to accommodate. Last night. A shudder ran through her as various scenes forced themselves into her mind. Last night had been a graphic illustration of what was missing from her life, and she had spent the greater part of the day confidently predicting a change in her lifestyle.

And yet . . . and yet if he had been willing, and she had absolutely no reason to imagine he hadn't been, what was there to stop her repeating what had happened last night? To put it crudely, what was to stop her using Patrick Cavour just as she was planning to use other men? Yes, and to be used by them—she wasn't foolish enough to ignore that aspect of such a relationship. As she had once heard in a corny old film, why settle for a penny candle when you could reach for the moon?

Ah, well, films were one thing, but now, after seeing him, even after having that stand-up row with him, she knew it was all wishful thinking. She was no more free now to exploit, to keep her emotional life separate, than she had been all those years ago. Less, in fact, much, much less, for last night had been clear proof that she had never quite escaped. And now she was forced to ask herself if it had all been worth it, for pride certainly didn't keep you warm at night. How bitter to begin to recognise the perfect scenario just about five years too late.

CHAPTER FIVE

AT LEAST that was one worry she could dismiss from her mind. Vigorously Leigh cleaned her teeth, wide eyes scrutinising her reflection in the bathroom mirror, wondering why she didn't feel a more positive sense of relief.

Her head was hidden by a white towel wrapped turban-style about her newly shampooed hair. Possibly that was why she looked so woebegone, but it certainly wasn't due to the time of the month. It was... Hastily she turned away, went to the bedroom and took a moment plugging in the hairdrier. It was almost as if there was some half-buried disappointment that she didn't, after all, find herself pregnant with Patrick Cavour's child.

Incredible. She made a lukewarm attempt to laugh at herself. For the three days since that awful scene with him she had been desperately worried, toying with all sorts of impractical plans, wondering how her parents would react—with dismay and disappointment, that was one certainty. She knew other women who had chosen to bring up children on their own, but when she had visualised herself in the mother role there had always been some man there alongside her. Impatient with herself, she carelessly dragged at a strand of hair. Oh, why not be completely

honest...? *One* man by her side—not some man.
Always the same man...

That, of course, could explain a lot. Her questioning violet eyes were shadowy with pain. Had she, perhaps, been harbouring a secret fantasy of confronting Patrick, telling him that in spite of her earlier assurances she *did* find that she was expecting his child, and what did he suggest they should do?

It wasn't, *was not*, as if she had had any idea that he might suggest marriage. Of course not. Even if they had been in a permanent relationship she would neither have expected nor wished for such a thing, but... He would most likely have been frightfully decent and correct, would have assured her that she need not worry, that he would assume full responsibility, that she need have no worries about finances and...

Tears stung unexpectedly at her eyes. She blinked several times and sniffed. And naturally it would have given her enormous pleasure to refuse, to say that of course she would manage perfectly, that she was informing him solely because he had been so insistent about it.

In an effort at distraction she ran her fingers through her hair approvingly. What a relief to be self-approving for once, to like the way it shone with cleanliness, the way it floated softly about her head. She shrugged off her towelling robe and reached for her clean things. Anyway, it *was* a great relief to consign that particular worry to history. Tonight she planned to go to the nearest bistro and eat a pleasant meal. A pity she would be on her own—she had thought of calling Holly, but there was no way she was going to risk an invitation to that particular apartment...

When the telephone shrilled, she jumped, sighed when she realised how shot to pieces her nerves were, and walked into the hallway to pick up the receiver.

'Oh, Kyle.' It was a relief to hear her employer's voice. 'I didn't expect—— Is there anything wrong?'

'Nothing at all, love. I just wondered...I had to come to Paris unexpectedly, and now I find I have the evening free. I'm booked back on a late flight but I wondered—can I persuade you to take pity on me and come out to dinner? There's a new place I've just heard of, should be worth a visit, and you know I always hate the idea of eating alone. So, how about it?'

'Oh, Kyle.' Her immediate reaction was reluctance. 'I was just about to pop down to Verdier's on the corner.'

'Change your mind! The place I have in mind is an old mill-house on the river; on a balmy evening like this it must be worth going to. You could bring me up to date on the last few days and I promise to get you back before midnight.'

'I'd rather bring you up to date during working hours, if you don't mind, and I would like to be back here long before midnight, but...' She wavered, knowing instinctively that the worst thing for her in her present mood would be too much of her own undiluted company.

'Go on.' Sensing her weakening, he pressed his advantage. 'You shall come home the moment it suits you.'

'And you promise you won't talk shop?'

'I promise. Thanks, Leigh; I'll pick you up in about thirty minutes.' And he rang off, leaving her wondering why she had given in so easily.

However, when they reached the small, elegant restaurant, having strolled across beautifully clipped turf to the little terrace on the banks of the Seine, and when they had lingered a while over clinking glasses of Campari and soda, she found that her mood was very nearly mellow.

It was a positive relief not to be dining on her own, and Kyle was just the kind of undemanding male companion who suited the occasion. They got on well together, and if at one time he had rather given the impression that their relationship could develop into something warmer, at least he had quickly picked up the message that she wasn't into entanglements with married men and had moved on. There were rumours about him and a number of his colleagues, but she had never troubled to find out if they were true. Now his manner towards her was that of a good friend as well as employer, and that suited both of them.

Another plus was that the prospect of dinner in a smart restaurant had forced her to take a little more trouble with her appearance, which meant that her morale had risen slightly. At least, she was confident that the aquamarine shirt suited her and the navy patterned skirt wasn't too casual. Round her neck she had linked a short string of glass beads, blue shot through in a variety of shades, which gave the entire outfit a lift.

'Ah.' When he had come into the flat to collect her, Kyle had allowed an appreciative gaze to skim over her. 'You're looking better.' He had smiled amiably. 'I was beginning to worry about you.'

'You needn't.' Her tone had been very slightly sharp, possibly because she had known he was right. There *had* been shadows beneath her eyes—too many sleepless nights, she imagined—but it was amazing what a few moments with paint and powder could do to restore one's credibility. And a good blast of that delicious perfume she had bought the other day.

Inside the restaurant, amazingly busy for an evening mid-week, they were shown to a large round table with four place-settings, two of which were speedily whisked away. A waiter flicked once or twice at the immaculate pink linen before they were seated and offered menus.

'Mmm.' Realising she was very hungry, Leigh studied the list with interest. 'Clever of you to find this place, Kyle. Who told you about it?'

'Hmm? What?' He glanced across at her. 'Oh... must have been someone in Strasbourg. I can't remember exactly who, but you know how interested they all are in food.'

'I am too, right now. And I've made up my mind.' She laid aside her menu, waited while Kyle had a conference with the waiter, then gave her order. 'I suppose Anna is still in Strasbourg?'

'Anna?' For just a split-second the comment, casual as it was, appeared to throw him. 'Yes, so far as I know. Though at this time in the evening——' he glanced at his watch and shrugged '—who knows?'

'Mmm. I confess I'm not sure what she does in her free time.' First courses arrived, napkins were shaken out, draped across knees. 'We meet from time to time, but since we live at opposite ends of the town...'

'Don't let it get cold.' Kyle held out a huge pepper-mill.

'This——' she savoured the first mouthful of asparagus '—is absolutely heavenly.'

'I'm glad. It would have been an awful let-down if the food had been disappointing after all I'd been told.'

'No chance of that.'

They were just starting on the main course of duckling when Kyle looked up with an expression of surprise and... and something else, too instantly veiled to be identified, as he recognised who had just come in.

'Inés.' His voice was neutral, indicating neither interest nor pleasure, but it was impossible for Leigh to forget how consistently their names had been linked at one time. But then wasn't that true of practically every presentable female employed at the Palais de l'Europe?

Preparing her own expression to one of friendliness, she looked up, but the smile on her lips froze as her eyes were drawn beyond, to the man whose hand was placed so protectively on the Spanish woman's elbow. And the expression in Patrick Cavour's eyes as he returned her look was stony with indifference, so cold, in fact, that conversely Leigh was incandescent with fury.

But that didn't stop her habit of registering so many meaningless details—the dark suit, single-breasted so that it showed off the tall, powerful figure, the broad shoulders of the sportsman, the narrow waist... God...

Without her realising, her fingers began to play nervously with the blue beads... She would never forget the first time at Loughskerrie, when she had seen him on that enormous black gelding with the raking stride, more the Centaur of ancient myth than two distinct animals. It had been later that same day—such memories, once set in train, could not be aborted—that he had taken her off in to the Wicklow Hills, mounted in front of him, one arm pulling her taut back against him... The images were insistent, doubtless made more forceful by her recent entanglement. She was back in that secret dell, lying on the moss, soft and deep as a feather-bed, while Patrick...

No... She dropped her fork with a clatter, smiled a wan apology to Kyle... *No*. This time she thought she had hold of her treacherous thoughts. This was madness; if anyone were to guess—if *he* were to guess...

She forced herself back to the present, struggling against waves of heat, determined to make her smile convincing, but surely her expressive eyes, wide and panic-stricken, must have be-

trayed dismay when she realised that arrange-
ments were being made for the other two to join
them. Even now the waiter was rearranging
things; cutlery and glasses were being replaced...

'I do hope we're not intruding?' Inés—and it
was a small relief—had been placed opposite
Leigh and was being all charm. 'I can't understand how there could have been such a mistake
when I booked last week.'

Last week? Leigh forced her stiff lips into a
smile. So, last week, when she and Patrick had
been...together...this dinner had already been
arranged. Applying herself to rapidly congealing
duck, she found that her appetite had disappeared; even the tiniest slivers she could swallow
only with difficulty.

As always, it was best to concentrate on the
mundane. Inés was the essence of chic good taste:
a dress in dark red silk emphasised the slightly
voluptuous figure which might—oh, the relief of
uncharitable thoughts—run slightly to fat in
middle age, but which in the meantime would
cause most men to drool. The glossy black hair
was coiled into its usual knot, which in spite of
its severity seemed so right for her exotic style...

Leigh's attention was diverted when she
became aware of Patrick's fixed stare. She directed a flicking sideways glance in his direction,
hoping he might pick up on her disapproval, but
if he did he certainly gave no sign. His swift,
chilly assessment swept over her in an instant,
then, with a narrowing of his eyes, it moved to
her companion. And back again. That con-

temptuous searing expression told her as clearly as if he had spelled it out that he was coming to some conclusion, solving some problem...

And then her mind focused on Kyle, and the penny dropped. Of course. He was putting two and two together and making a complete mess of the answer. How dared he? she thought angrily. How *dared* he assume that she would choose someone like her employer, a married man, whose reputation was...? Especially when *he* was escorting a woman like Inés da Silva. How dared he judge? Oh, if only she could summon an equally opinionated expression then he would be under no illusions...

And even if she and Kyle were... But on the other hand—and it was little comfort to remember—wasn't this exactly the impression she had been so keen to convey? So what had she to complain about...? It could hardly have worked better if it had been carefully planned, only...it hurt so much having him thinking—— She pulled her thoughts up short.

Now he and Inés were ordering, the Spanish woman leaning over to Patrick, one hand, with lots of rings and red nails, placed intimately on his dark sleeve as they discussed the menu. She said something in a voice too low to catch, and when he laughed Leigh was stabbed by jealousy. That deep, intimate sound; once she had imagined it was for her alone... She pulled herself together. What fools we are, we women, she thought, allowing ourselves to be taken in...

It was a relief when Kyle spoke, forcing her attention, though it was to Patrick that his remarks were directed. 'So it looks as if you'll be getting quite a large grant for your cause, Patrick. I think we were all impressed by the forceful way you put your case to the committee.'

'I *hope* it will be successful.' His sudden grin and shrug dismissed his own efforts. 'Not my cause, as such—my company has simply been retained by the agency.'

'But of course you're being modest.' Inés smiled admiringly at her companion. 'You, Kyle, know well enough, but perhaps you don't, Leigh, that Patrick spent a long time on the ground with an aid project.'

Fortunately there was no need for Leigh to say anything since Kyle was doing it for her. 'Yes, and of course that makes all the difference. It shows you have some idea of just what you're talking about—rare enough in our circles.' He changed tack. 'You didn't find it a handicap, then, taking time out on your career for several years?'

'No.' After a pause, while he and Inés were served, he looked up briefly, then, taking up his fork, broke off a piece of salmon. 'The reverse, if anything. I don't think experience of that kind is ever a handicap. In the end it comes down to confidence, I suppose.'

As if, thought Leigh sourly, any Cavour had ever lacked *that* quality. Then she allowed her thoughts to wander, only vaguely picking up phrases like 'life-enhancing experience' and 'the cultural density of life' as they floated about her. She was even aware of her own voice, throwing in the occasional uncontroversial bland remark from time to time—the kind of comments a robot might as easily have produced.

All of a sudden she started as Kyle, quite unexpectedly, put out his hand and touched hers, asking in a manner that was almost protective, 'Am I neglecting you, love? Tell me what you would like next. Cheese? Dessert? I've been told the *tarte aux pommes* is something of an experience.'

'Not another thing, Kyle.' Now all she wanted was to be done with the evening; she wanted to be on her own and preferably in bed. 'I've had a wonderful dinner and——'

'Good. Two coffees.' He spoke to the hovering waiter and then to the other two. 'I promised to get Leigh back to the flat before midnight.'

'The flat?' Inés raised a very slender black eyebrow, glancing curiously at Leigh, who was giving all her attention to a young woman at the next table, trying to be impervious to Patrick Cavour's thunderous expression.

'Mmm. I have some business interests in Paris, and it seemed sensible to have a flat rather than pay astronomical hotel bills. We stay there when we come here on private business.'

'But...' The arrival of the coffee robbed Leigh of the chance to explain that they never came together, and that if Kyle had unwittingly given the impression that they were both going back there tonight, then . . . But when the waiter had gone, the conversation had moved on, and the explanation would surely have enhanced rather than allayed any suspicions which he . . . which they might have had.

She drank quickly, then reached pointedly for her handbag, and to her relief Kyle took the hint. 'If you'll excuse us? I promised to take Leigh to see the moon rise over the Seine . . .'

What on earth was the man trying to do? Leigh looked at him irritably. Was he trying to make them think . . . ?

'In that case——' when she chose, Inés could be quite acid '—I hope you have your rose-tinted spectacles. I doubt you'll see it otherwise.'

'Ah, Inés.' Kyle shook his head in mocking disappointment. 'Ever the realist.' He pushed back his chair and stood. 'But Leigh is a true romantic, and has every confidence in my promises, so——' there was a long moment while he and Inés looked at each other '—don't disillusion her, please.'

And before she would have thought it possible they were outside in the warm evening, walking slowly down the path towards the river. Kyle, after asking her permission, lit up a cigar.

'Mmm. He's a good-looking young man. And very astute. Seems to me he gets right to the heart of things.'

'He *is* pretty well-qualified, after all.' The words came out before Leigh could stop them.

'Ah.' He draped a friendly arm about her shoulder. 'So you *do* know something about him. I did wonder... And yet... that night at the reception I got the distinct impression that you didn't know him.'

'It is quite a long time since we last saw each other, and...'

'Neither of you, I suggest, would be easily forgotten. Tell me, Leigh——' for a moment he held her at arm's length, staring down through narrowed eyes '—are you blushing?'

'Of course not,' she lied. 'It's just... But you are right. I do know Patrick Cavour—used to, at least. Slightly.'

'Ah, slightly. And yet I felt I was picking up some powerful vibrations...'

'Well, as I said, it was such a long time ago.' Why on earth had she embarked on this senseless deceit? 'When I was a student he appeared at Oxford to do some research. That was when I met him.'

There was a longish silence before Kyle prompted quite gently, 'And then...?'

'Then nothing. It was just that I heard he had been to Harvard Law School, and after that he worked with an American firm of attorneys. So, you see, he would know his way around.'

'Yes.' Kyle pursed his lips. 'So it would appear. Now what, I wonder, would bring him to Europe after seeming to be so successfully settled in the States?'

'I couldn't say.' No point in explaining further, especially when the question he was asking was one she had pondered through many sleepless nights. It had crossed her mind that he might have discovered where she was working and had followed her, but since she was certain he had been as shocked as she was that night there was little point in tormenting herself with a fictional scenario complete with sugary romantic ending. 'I suppose Inés might have more detail on that than I have...' Jealousy was like a knife-blade. 'They did look——' now she was being spiteful as certain ideas flitted into her mind '—remarkably friendly, don't you think?' Then she said, before he could answer, 'Didn't you find it an amazing coincidence, Inés appearing there the very time we were there? The odds against that happening must be considerable.'

'Oh, I don't know.' He shrugged, drew deeply on the cigar, then blew the smoke away from her. 'It happens all the time in Strasbourg. There it is difficult to avoid people you know.'

'Strasbourg, yes, that's understandable—but Paris...' She frowned, more puzzled by the random encounter now than she had been at first. 'Who was it told you about this place, Kyle? Can you remember?'

'I think it might have been Charles Sebastien.' He frowned. 'Yes, I'm almost sure, and maybe... Yes, there was a group of us at the time, and I'm pretty positive Inés was there too. So there you are——' he grinned '—mystery solved.'

'Mmm.' She was unconvinced. 'I must remember to ask Inés next time I see her.' But her threat, if it was that, left him unmoved.

'You do that,' he said cheerily, stubbed out his cigar in a flowerpot and began to lead her back along the riverbank in the direction of the car park. 'I'm sure she'll confirm what I've said—if you think it's important, I mean.'

The balmy evening, the idyllic setting were soothing after the fraught time spent inside, and although there was no moon concealed lights along the sides of the path cast shimmering reflections across the water and made it quite seductive. There were secret sheltered corners, arbours tucked away amid scrambling roses, even a tiny dovecote—crumbling, picturesque, immaculate—offering privacy to passing lovers. Yes, it was all very pretty, could have been romantic given the right companion. What a pity Kyle did not fit the role. The very idea caused a wan smile. Even if he hadn't a long-standing marriage with a particularly charming woman he would never have compared with... with anyone she had ever... ever dated.

But at least he was concerned about her, concerned and certainly non-threatening—very nearly paternal—so that when they stopped at a tiny spit of land, stood for a moment to watch the powerful current and he put his arm about her shoulder again, she didn't, with her normal good sense, move casually away. Instead she gave a shuddering sigh, deep and wearied, leaning against him in momentary weakness.

'Something is making you sad, Leigh. I've noticed it for some time.'

'No, truly, Kyle. Nothing at all.' But his sympathy brought the sting of tears to her eyes, and an unexpected sob was wrenched from her throat. Eyes wide, she shook her head, till a hand beneath her chin forced her to be still and to look into his concerned face.

'A man?' His voice was gently teasing. 'None of us is worth it, you know.' His smile was cynical and self-mocking. 'Take it from an expert in the field.'

'I'm sorry, Kyle.' Hastily she reached into her bag for a handkerchief. 'Just as well there's no moon—I could have blamed that.' It was an effort even to pretend to be light-hearted, impossible to explain why she was feeling so desperately weepy.

'But since there's no moon...'

'Don't worry about it, Kyle. I promise it's nothing but a touch of *Weltschmerz*, and I also promise it will in no way affect my work.' And to put an end to the discussion, and entirely on impulse, she leaned forward and dropped a light kiss on his cheek, not considering what his reaction might be.

It was precisely the reaction she ought to have expected. And one Patrick Cavour had all the time in the world to observe as he sauntered along the main path with his companion. For, while she was being accommodated into the welcoming curve of Kyle Lessor's body, Leigh, stunned into quiescence, was looking directly at the taller man.

For a moment she burned with the humiliation of the situation, then the blood seemed to leave her head. She was weak and giddy, clinging to Kyle from necessity rather than passion. It was the expression in Patrick's eyes, the distaste in his manner which were so destructive, both, in spite of distance and darkness, easy to interpret and owing nothing to her imagination, entirely consistent with his legal training. She was being charged, tried and convicted, and had little doubt that the sentence would be exacted with all the severity that the law allowed.

They were, it seemed to her, cut off from their companions. Inés, just a step behind Patrick, appeared to be watching something further down the river, and Kyle... Well, she had always known he was a typical opportunist male—what else?— and he was murmuring comforting words in her ear which she certainly had no desire to listen to...

Close at hand she heard a sudden plop, as if a fish had broken the surface of the water, but she knew it was something else. She alone had seen Patrick Cavour's scorn as he'd tossed a pebble into the river. For a moment she looked at the shimmering reflections on the surface and then, disengaging herself abruptly from Kyle's embrace, she looked up to see Patrick following something Inés was pointing out to him. Their heads were very close together and her hand was possessively resting on his arm.

They were walking away, Inés chatting with great animation. The entire scene, Leigh thought bleakly, as she and Kyle resumed their stroll, might have been a final comment on her relationship with Patrick. It was as insubstantial and illusory as that.

CHAPTER SIX

THERE was no earthly reason for Leigh to go overboard for the christening. A new hat was understandable, but she had several scarcely worn outfits which would have served the purpose perfectly. Yes, she conceded, the ceremony *was* being held in Paris and, yes, all sorts of fashionable people would be there... But no! Tears made her eyes sting at the very suggestion which would not stay at the back of her mind where it belonged. *No*, it was nothing to do with Patrick Cavour, for heaven's sake. Nothing whatsoever. But not all the vehemence in the world was totally reassuring.

It was the hat which was the key to the whole outfit. A black silk velour *bombe*, glossy as a guardsman's busby and with a spotted eye-veil, it was vampish and entirely irresistible, and from the instant the milliner had placed it on her head at that perfect angle she hadn't tried to resist.

With the suit it was sensational. The curvy jacket was sunflower-yellow with a black rouleau trim, not one of her usual colours, but this—short-sleeved, nipped-in, showing her slender waist—was very chic, entirely French. The black skirt that went with it was short—certainly much shorter than anything else in her wardrobe, and with flattish black pumps—she didn't want to

tower too spectacularly over Holly and Paul—
black gloves and handbag, well, she couldn't remember when she had last been so excited by her
own reflection. At least... it must have been when
she had set off for the reception, and then, she
thought with complete irrelevance, she had had
no idea about whom she was going to meet.

She gave a last confirming glance towards the
hotel mirror, checking her seams were straight,
her make-up as good as she could manage. In
fact she had been rather light-handed—just a flick
of powder, a touch of lipstick, a little more
positive with the eyes, wide and luminous beneath the veil, her eyelids shadowy with a colour
which called itself Wild Sloe... She turned away
impatiently, suspicious of such unusual self-
regard, then, almost defiantly, blasted herself
with some new perfume, adjusted the hat frac-
tionally and left.

Arriving at Holly's flat, she was enveloped by
a whirl of friends and relatives. She wished, not
for the first time, that she had persisted with her
original plan to meet up with them at the church.
It would have been as easy to take her taxi there
instead, simpler for everyone, and...

'So we've arranged for Patrick to take you to
the church, Leigh.'

'What?' About to sip from the coffee-cup
which had been thrust into her hand, Leigh
looked at her friend in consternation. 'But
Holly...'

'No buts. I promise you, he doesn't mind a
bit. He's an absolute sweetie, and when we asked

of course he said yes. A quick glance in the mirror might give some explanation for such an attitude. But now, have we covered every point? When we reach the font I hand Pauli over to you, and then ...'

Leigh released her mind into a fevered spin, entirely oblivious of all the finer points of the day's ceremony which Holly was so painstakingly itemising. She must just rely on past experience to take her safely through the ceremony. It was so obvious now—all the recent days when she had been struggling to keep calm, Holly, it seemed, had been doing her best to undermine her resolve ... had been busy with all sorts of plans. It was hard to excuse such persistent disloyalty from one she had previously regarded as a friend. Couldn't she see the kind of threat ...?

'Good, then that's all clear. Now, we'd better think about getting off—the last thing we want is to be late.' Holly giggled excitedly. 'I'll just give Patrick a ring, let him know you're waiting, then see if Pauli is ready for his big occasion.'

And, of course—wouldn't you know it?—he— Patrick, that was—was enough to knock your eyes out.

In an effort to simplify matters Leigh had taken to the corridor, walking up and down in a desperate search for calm—very difficult when memories of her last time in the building would keep intruding. So many disturbing images would not keep to the shadows where they belonged.

Then came the soft whirr of machinery, a jolt in her stomach like the kick from a mule, the clunk of opening doors... She felt light-headed, slightly sick; her neck was much too weak to support the weight of that ridiculous hat, and her heart quite simply turned over in her chest when he stepped out and they stood looking at each other.

And she, stricken with panic, tongue cleaving to the roof of her mouth, was unable to do more than contemplate. And admire. Reluctantly. But it would have been impossible to do otherwise.

Perfectly tailored suit—conservative, as she would have expected for a formal occasion—dark grey, but relieved from dullness by a faint red stripe, white shirt and dashing tie in tiny black and white check. In the buttonhole he wore a single pink rose. Just like—the recollection caught at her heart—like the one he had worn that other night in Oxford. Not, of course, that it would have been intended as a reminder.

Aware of being caught gazing, afraid that her appreciation might have been blatantly displayed, she summoned a strained and determined-to-be-casual smile. 'Patrick. Sorry to impose on you yet again. I gather you've been appointed to act as my chauffeur. You must be tiring of that role.'

To that there was no reply, certainly none of the automatic denial which common courtesy demanded. Merely a raised eyebrow—might that be an accusation of hypocrisy?—a faint smile and a glance at his watch. Just a glimpse of heavy gold cuff-links and she had an urge, foolish but incredibly powerful, simply to touch the back of his hand, to feel the spring of hair under her fingertips ...

'We ought to be off. Beat the rush.' A gesture ushered her ahead of him into the lift and a moment later they were dropping silently to the underground garage.

It was a quiet car journey too, although his naturally impeccable manners were in evidence. The door was held open for her—he appeared not even to notice her embarrassment as she struggled with the skirt rising way above her knees—and the seatbelt was dealt with before the door was firmly slammed shut.

There were one or two remarks about the lightness of the Sunday traffic, about the type of car he was driving, but it was just minutes before they were parking in the quiet square, climbing the wide flight of steps to the church. She felt another quiver in the pit of her stomach when his fingers grazed her bare elbow as he guided her into the quiet serenity of the ancient building.

Afterwards, all her recollections of the ceremony were bound up with Patrick Cavour. The central purpose of the day dissolved into the recesses of her mind, although it was a great relief afterwards to discover that she had done what was required of her, adequately if not impeccably.

But when she took the infant into her arms, smoothing the extravagantly fringed shawl, it was Patrick's concentrated attention she was aware of, into his sombre intent eyes that she looked each time she raised her head... Had he noticed? she wondered. Whenever she flicked back her lashes they touched the veil, causing a tiny nervy throb...and for some reason her heart was racing too—wildly, loudly so that she was half convinced that the entire congregation must hear and be wondering—and her legs were weak, so weak that she thought they might give way from sheer emotion. And if they did, what would happen? she speculated. Would Patrick perhaps attempt a saving dive for the infant, reaching him just in time? Once at a varsity rugger match she had seen him successfully scoop the ball and go on to make a winning try...

Please—she raised expressive eyes to look at him across the font—please help me. And, as if he understood, his expression softened, grew encouraging—at least, she imagined so—as she heard her own voice, in response to the queries from the American pastor, giving the expected answers.

Then it was his turn. Pauli was transferred by his mother from Leigh's arms to Patrick's and no one, seeing the expert way he settled the child in the crook of his arm, the soothing way he patted him when for an instant the child seemed unsettled, could fail to be impressed. And deeply affected. Then the voice, firm and confident, with the same promise that would always send shivers down her spine.

When his eyes returned to hers guilty colour stained her skin as she realised for the first time, how intent, maybe even hungry, her manner had been, and that was all to do with the dream her mind had been fixed on. No, not that other one, though there was an indisputable connection; this was a daydream in which, had things worked out differently, they were at their own child's christening. For a few delicious moments she had been back at Loughskerrie, in that lovely Georgian house, and surrounded by all those exuberant, friendly Cavours, with his parents and hers celebrating the baptism of a grandchild.

The pain of it, and the joy, was a torment. Numbly she watched as he handed the child back to his mother, and the dream faded simultaneously. She and Patrick returned to their seats, and they even shared a prayer book for the final responses, his voice firm and melodious, hers, to her own ears, thin and shaky, wholly lacking in confidence.

There was relief in getting back to the flat and the buffet luncheon produced by caterers. There she could quite easily detach herself; she need never speak another word to him if that was how she felt, not even goodbye, though that would be easy, she decided balefully. She was free to mingle, to chat and laugh with other guests, to enjoy herself, for heaven's sake, which was surely one of the purposes of the occasion and which she hadn't done so far, thanks to him. It was even possible that their views on that would coincide.

And as it happened there were several men present who seemed more than willing to help her do just that. One in particular, an American who told her he had been at college with Paul, insisted on exchanging telephone numbers with her, in spite of the fact that she couldn't summon the energy to offer any encouragement.

Possibly that was because she was too interested in what was happening at the other side of the room, where Patrick, lounging against the wall directly in her line of vision, seemed to have appropriated the two most attractive women present for his own personal pleasure. And theirs—she determined to be fair. Oh, yes, and theirs.

Cautiously sipping the ice-cold champagne, eyes only vaguely fixed in a certain direction, she drifted casually across, exchanging a word here and there until she was almost within earshot. The taller of the two women, the one with the stunning auburn hair rippling to her shoulders, was another American; she couldn't catch the accent of the other, who was less flamboyant but, she guessed, more Patrick's type.

A joyful burst of laughter from the trio forced her to raise her head disapprovingly, and at that very moment Patrick glanced her way. She felt herself begin to colour as his smile faded; his words confirmed that he was aware of her curiosity.

'Don't stand on the fringe, Leigh.' How dared he imply...? 'Let me introduce you to Paul's cousin and a friend from LA.' And he completed the introductions while she simmered quietly, barely giving her time to take in their names. And then almost at once his presence was required elsewhere and she was left, mind totally blank, unable to think of a sensible thing to say.

'You know Patrick well, Leigh?' The redhead was following him with her eyes, and Leigh found that she was doing the same.

'Well?' She considered. 'I can't say I know him well, exactly.' How easily lies came tripping from the tongue. 'I met him—oh, some time ago.'

'Some time ago?' the woman queried in a gently mocking tone. 'You must be spoiled with attractive men if you don't remember precisely. *I* can remember precisely—date, time, place— where I first met him.'

'Oh?' It seemed safer to make no further enquiries about that, and in any case a few more guests had joined them and the conversation moved on, but she couldn't rid herself of awareness of him, even when she deliberately turned her back.

A little later she saw that the redhead had cornered him again—or had it been the other way round? Whatever, she was sparkling wildly and he was lapping it up. A sudden unwelcome vision came into her mind. She saw that beautiful Titian hair spread out on pillows—how seductive... You could hardly blame a man for... Oh, damn it.

Firmly she turned and walked from the room. She was mad, persevering with this self-torture; let them do what they wanted—it was nothing to her what he did. With Inés da Silva or itinerant Americans, she simply didn't care, and the pain that was tearing at her was bound to ease soon.

But it was impossible to escape for long. Soon Holly winkled her out. 'You must come, love; the speeches are about to begin and I think Paul is going to say nice things about you.' So she was ushered willy-nilly to that end of the room, forced to smile at the flattering references, which naturally included both godparents, and with Patrick standing close enough to touch it took all her powers of self-control.

After all the more obvious toasts there was one to the godparents, and she and Patrick had no choice but to turn to each other, glasses raised, hypocritical smiles in place, while a few camera bulbs flashed. She imagined it was as unwelcome to him as it was to her. Only by fixing her eyes firmly on a pattern on the wallpaper, just to the left of his shoulder, was she able to preserve an appearance of detachment and enjoyment. But the moment the formality was over she turned abruptly and sought the solace of the nursery.

Soon there were sounds of guests leaving. Her sense of relief and release was enormous, and she emerged from the nursery just as Holly crossed the hall and began to make her excuses. 'He refuses to wake up for his godmother.' She smiled and shrugged philosophically. 'So I'm having to hope that tomorrow things will be better.'

'Oh, love, do you have to go away so soon?'

'I think I should—and you still have your relatives with you. If it's still all right I'll come round in the morning. You do remember I said I wasn't going back till late afternoon? We can have a real heart to heart then. Provided——' she raised an eyebrow in the direction of her host, who had just come forward to join them '—provided Paul III assures me he'll have returned to his money-bags by then.'

'You're making me regret the important meeting I have at nine-thirty. I would much rather listen to you two letting your hair down.'

'But that would spoil all the fun, wouldn't it?' Holly kissed her friend on both cheeks. 'And thank you, Leigh, for being such a perfect god-mother. In fact——' she turned to her husband for confirmation '——if we had searched the length and breadth of the country we couldn't have found better-looking godparents.'

'I'll settle for the glamorous godmother,' Paul draped an arm round his wife's shoulders. 'And that hat—it's been the talk of the afternoon.'

'Oh, yes, the hat.' Leigh wrinkled her nose. 'That reminds me—I left it in the nursery. I'd better go and pick it up.'

There she and Holly found that Pauli was being fed, and somehow Leigh was holding him again, while the girl who was helping consulted his mother about some little adjustments to his cot. She even found she was enjoying it. His cheek against hers was so incredibly soft, the tiny fingers were reaching out to catch her hair, and she propped him against her shoulder, walked up and down once or twice, rubbing his back in what she thought was the approved way.

She had no idea she was being watched till she passed a mirrored cupboard, and she stopped abruptly as she stared into the unwavering eyes of Patrick Cavour. For just a moment she was transfixed, paralysed by the rush, the deluge of emotions which tore at her senses . . . Something in his eyes added to her pain—a slight frown, an expression which made her long to rush forward, say something—anything that might begin to soothe . . .

'Here, Leigh, let me.' Holly smiled as she appropriated her son. 'Leaving you all this time . . .' Then they walked into the hall to find—of course; she might have guessed—Paul with Patrick by the door. 'It's all arranged. Patrick volunteered to see you back, Leigh. He doesn't mind a bit.' Holly grinned at Patrick and lowered her voice confidentially. 'Leigh imagines you have to be coerced into offering to take her anywhere. As if any normal male wouldn't jump at the chance.'

Too incensed to say anything, Leigh remained silent until they were in the elevator and then, hoping her voice wouldn't show exactly how furious she felt, said, 'I'd be grateful, Patrick——' thank heavens she sounded cool and detached '—if we could stop at the concierge's office. I can call a cab from there. There's no reason for you to get your car out again.'

'If that's what you want.'

For an instant she was shocked—in spite of apparently getting her own way, she had not expected him to give in so easily. If not an argument at least he might have gone through the motions, however insincere.

'Best thing——' Patrick interrupted her thoughts '—would be to call from my apartment. The concierge is often having a break about now.'

So she found herself following him along the corridor, hesitating outside his door, then stepping reluctantly into the hallway, watching as he crossed to the telephone alcove.

'You know...' He had begun to dial a number, and for a moment she was too involved with her roused emotions to realise that it was to her he was speaking. She swung round from the water-colour she had been examining so intently. 'You have a mark down the back of that beautiful jacket you're wearing.' She watched the receiver being replaced, aware as he came towards her that her heart was beating madly in her chest, that if he should touch her she couldn't guarantee what her reaction would be... 'If you would like to take it off I could try...'

'Oh, yes?' Thank goodness she had found the strength to smile with cynical disbelief.

'It looks——' his voice was clipped, matter-of-fact and crushing '—very much like milk.'

'Oh.' For an instant she was taken aback, then it began to register how she had taken the baby, soothing him against her shoulder, and wasn't regurgitation one of their favourite pastimes in those circumstances? 'Oh,' she said again, this time shaking her head in faint resignation.

'If you would like to give me your jacket, I'll do my best to clean it.'

'Thank you.' She undid the buttons, slipping the jacket from her shoulders and handing it to him, conscious that her brief camisole top was more than a little provocative. Only, she wasn't going to allow him to imagine that she was nervous, that she was afraid of her own reactions, and besides . . . she had herself to convince as well . . . She followed him to the kitchen—all gleaming navy units, shining steel and smoky glass—watching as he dealt quickly and efficiently with the dribble, finishing off with a slightly damp cloth, rubbing it with a clean tea-towel and then offering it to her.

'There you are. I don't think there's any permanent damage and it's not damp enough to cause rheumatics.' He watched impassively as she shrugged herself back into the garment, fastening it with shaking fingers, and she was very relieved, so she told herself, that no decision was required of her. She had been so certain—afraid, rather, she corrected herself quickly—afraid that events might have been conspiring to lead her in *that* direction, although it was something of an anticlimax to discover that there was no need to fight him off, that he was apparently as unwilling as she was to resume . . .

'There *was* something else . . .' He left her. She followed as far as the hall but waited outside the bedroom, looking at him when he returned, still suspicious. He had something concealed in one hand and this was held out towards her; she found herself looking at the blue necklace she had worn when she was out with Kyle.

'Yours, I think.' He was unsmiling, accusing enough to bring heat burning into her face.

'Yes, thank you. I realised I had lost it when I got back to the flat.'

'I found it beside your chair and recognised it.'

'Oh, I see.' She slipped it into her pocket. 'It isn't worth anything but it's pretty, and I'm glad to have it back.'

'You don't mind going round with married men?' Now he was coldly stern and judgemental. How she hated people who never allowed others the benefit of the doubt.

'I'm sorry?' she frowned, halfway between anger and condescending amusement.

'I suggested——' now emotions were beginning to show and he spoke with force, through his teeth '—that you like to go about with married men.'

'And if I do?' Humiliation made her determined to strike back. 'Can you explain how it is any business of yours?'

'Only to the extent that I expected different standards from you.'

Seething now with barely controlled anger, she had to resist the inclination to spit out the words. 'By sheer chance I had dinner with Kyle Lessor, who just happens to be my boss. End of story. I suppose even you have at some time been taken out to dinner by your employer without attracting adverse comments?' Now she directed the anger towards herself, irritated that she was choosing to explain...

'What in this case attracts comment is that Kyle, for all his laid-back manner, has something of a reputation. From what I'm told he seems to be working his way through every available female in the Palais.'

'How *dare* you?'

He raised an eyebrow, clearly not following her train of thought.

'How dare you assume that I'm one of what you call "available" females at the Palais? I notice you never refer to men in that way, or is that——' her brilliant eyes sparkled with passionate resentment '—because men are always available?'

'Some undoubtedly are.' His anger was less apparent than hers, showing only in the tightness of the jaw, the clenched teeth and the narrowed eyes, though she had little doubt that it was equally intense. 'Everything I've heard about your employer inclines me to think of him as a philanderer, and——'

'I think you'll agree that I know him as well as anyone, with——'

'That is exactly what I'm afraid of.'

'*You*,' she said coldly, 'have no right to be afraid. But what I was going to say——' the idea had just come to her, and she grasped it eagerly '—was that I know him as well as anyone, with the possible exception of your companion of the other night.' She smiled sourly. 'Perhaps you ought to be interrogating Inés.'

'What is that supposed to mean?'

'I mean that rumour has it that Kyle and Inés da Silva had something pretty exciting going for them at one time.'

'I'm surprised you listen to idle gossip.' His expression seemed disapproving.

'Oh, I don't know, it can be quite diverting, and besides, in a place like Strasbourg it's rather difficult to avoid. And, from what you've just been saying, you aren't exactly averse to listening yourself. But then I expect her pillow-talk is careful to edit out any detail which concerns herself.' She couldn't imagine what had brought that phrase to her mind, much less what had brought the words to her lips. During the seemingly endless pause she had time enough to wish the words unsaid; they were so utterly tasteless, and, besides, if he should choose to probe beneath the surface, so revealing. Moreover, she didn't really think he was already embarked on an affair with Inés—did she?

'Being bitchy doesn't suit you, Leigh.'

'No?' If she had been in any other place, with any other company, she would have broken down then; she would have wept with sheer misery and frustration. But Patrick Cavour was the one man in the world who must never learn of her weaknesses. In front of him she must maintain an air of cool detachment and produce, if it was at all possible, a certain amused condescension. 'It might not suit me but, strangely enough, I find it most enjoyable.'

'I find that rather hard to believe, knowing you as I once did.'

At that she laughed, and remembered it later as a shrill and shaming sound, cheap and degrading. 'That was in a different life, Patrick, and maybe we've both changed—more than either of us would like to admit.'

'You're probably right.'

'Of course I'm right.' Again she felt close to tears, and felt she had no choice but to attack. 'You shouldn't be naïve enough to imagine that others have changed, for the worse in my case——' she flung that charge at him '—while you have remained your old sweet self. Unfortunately, not many of us do.'

'I don't think anyone who really knows me would ever describe me as naïve, and of course I accept what you say. But——' his voice mellowed, and there was a note of reflection which held her spellbound '—I hope you don't get the impression that I consider all the changes in you are for the worse.'

The wide violet eyes were watching carefully; she hardly dared to move.

'No, you have changed from a very pretty girl into a stunningly beautiful woman, and I don't think there's a man living who wouldn't, having seen you, want to make love to you...'

Aware of something happening to her, a softening which a few moments earlier would have seemed impossible, she still stared, her eyes dark and limpid.

'That's why it all seems...'

For a moment she was still too entranced by the first words to notice, then the final ones told her where he was leading, and she was instantly all sparky and defensive. 'Yes, it all seems...such a pity? Is that what you were going to say? Or perhaps——' she made a great play of serious consideration '—yes, sordid would have been a better choice, wouldn't you agree?'

His face was blank with anger now, she could tell that, and it gave her a fleeting moment of satisfaction. 'It looks as if you've made up your own mind, doesn't it?'

'Yes,' she said and, turning, picked up her hat and bag from where she had placed them earlier. 'Just as you have been doing. But now, if you would be kind enough to call a cab for me, I shall wait downstairs for it to arrive.' She went to the door and opened it. He made no move to stop her, allowing her to leave and walk out into the emotional wilderness.

CHAPTER SEVEN

IT WAS a blessing that she'd had this short time with Holly, Leigh decided as she sat back in the chair of the hotel lounge and stirred her coffee. There was nothing like a few hours' window-shopping in Paris, especially in the company of such a dedicated shopper as her friend, to take the edge off one's nervous tension.

'Now——' Holly drew her chair a little closer '—that's all about me and mine, and bless you for listening, love. It's been wonderful bringing you up to date on everything that's happened since I threw in the towel in Strasbourg. If anyone had told me then ... Well——' she shrugged and grinned '—I won't go into it all again, but finding Paul was just the last thing I was hoping for. In fact, as you know, I was quite off men, determined not to get involved again.'

'You've been lucky,' said Leigh, and she hurried to add, 'And so has Paul—very lucky.'

'Mmm.' There was a touch of complacency in the smile, but then Holly looked more speculatively towards her companion. 'But what about you, Leigh? When I left I honestly didn't expect to see you in the same old job and——' she hesitated '—if you don't mind my saying so, you don't seem your usual bright self.'

'I'm fine.' Leaning forward to help herself to more cream, Leigh turned her face towards the window, watching a pair of swans gliding across the surface of the small lake in the hotel grounds. 'Working hard.' Turning back, she smiled ruefully, stirred thoughtfully at her coffee. 'A bit tired, perhaps. There has been a bit of trouble in the office recently with——'

'Not Kyle again?' Holly spoke sharply. 'If he's being difficult then you really must do something...'

'No, of course it's not Kyle.' For some reason Leigh felt herself colouring up, doubtless giving all the wrong signals. 'He hasn't been a problem since the early days; he isn't the kind to persist when he knows there's no point.'

'Well...' Holly was not wholly convinced. 'I just remember what it was like. We're all assumed to be fair game and no one knows better than I do just how much misery can be caused...'

'Well, in this case, I declare my boss to be entirely innocent.'

'If you say so, I'll take your word for it. Reluctantly. So...?'

'Well, things in the office have been a bit overwhelming. We had trouble with a new computer and I'm wondering if I made a mistake in letting Kyle persuade me to take on his business interests. All this travel back and forward. I know I'm not stuck in a hotel when I come here but it still seems like living out of a suitcase.'

'You know you can always come and stay with us when you come to Paris, Leigh. We'd be——'

'Oh, no!' How vehement she sounded, and of course Holly would have no idea what she was suggesting ... She managed a smile. 'Bless you for asking, but I wouldn't dream of inflicting myself upon you. No, the flat is reasonably comfortable; it's just...'

'Sounds as if it's just that Kyle is expecting too much of you. Of course it suits him to unload all the boring details on you while he's raking in the money. Mind you, I hope you won't give it up, because I'm looking forward to seeing much more of you in the future. I missed you a lot when I left Strasbourg. No sympathetic shoulder to cry on.' She grinned, then pulled a face as she looked at her watch. 'But, sadly, I think I'll have to tear myself away. I promised to be back so Marie could get away.'

'Me too. I've got to get packed and out to the airport. But we'll meet again soon.'

'Thank you again,' Holly said later, getting out of the cab they had shared, 'for being such a wonderful godmother yesterday.'

'I loved doing it.' Leigh smiled. 'And I hope Paul likes that nightie.'

After that, it was back to Strasbourg, and for the next three weeks Leigh threw herself into work with the dedication of a zealot, emerging at the end if not cleansed, at least calm, and able to cope with the visit of a friend whom she had invited that Saturday evening.

It had been an inconvenience that Anna had failed to appear at the office, had, according to her landlady, been summoned to London. The result had been an increased workload for Leigh, with piles of additional typing and filing. When she had spoken to Kyle about the desirability of finding a temp he had seemed barely to hear, had given the impression of being lost in a private world, totally immersed in his own not very happy thoughts. Undoubtedly he had things on his mind just now. Several important matters, ones which affected his own constituents, were pending, so... she must just wait and hope that Anna would return as abruptly as she had left, and if not...

Anyway, the weekend had come as a relief. She was looking forward to Jane's visit. The fish for the main course had been easily prepared and the cheesecake—well, even if it failed to reach the professional standard of the glossy illustration, she had no doubt that it would taste fine.

The table in the corner by the window had been set with pretty mats and posies of flowers at each place and, in the centre, pink candles to tone with the linen. That, at least, could have measured up to a magazine illustration, and now there was nothing to do but enjoy a leisurely shower. Oh, but before that she would just pop a bottle of wine into the fridge...

She was in the midst of drying her hair when the doorbell shrilled, startling her. Sure for a

moment that she had misheard, she switched off
the drier, but there it was again. She felt a second's panic, till a quick glance at the bedside
clock confirmed that there was a good hour
before ... But whoever it was certainly wasn't in
a patient mood. The bell sounded again, so prolonged, so very peremptory that she stood still in
sudden panicky suspicion ... But that, of course,
was wildly unlikely.

Belting her robe more securely about her waist,
she walked to the door and opened it tentatively.
Eyes suddenly wide with shock, she went to slam
it shut, but Patrick Cavour put his hand flat
against it.

'No, don't do that.' It was an order, certainly
nothing as polite as a request, and in any case
quite unnecessary as she had instantly changed
her mind. It would be pointless and stupid not
to let him in. There was nothing to be afraid of
and this was an opportunity to convince him that
she wasn't. As well as to convince herself.

With a little gesture of resignation she walked
ahead of him into the sitting-room, and found
the courage to turn round to face him when she
reached the centre. She was about to enquire what
he wanted, in the most caustic tone she could
muster, but as she opened her mouth to speak
she found herself hesitating, taking time out
to ... just to look at him.

There was something unconsciously yearning
in the way her eyes absorbed and recorded every
detail of his appearance. Clothes, especially the
expensive casual clothes he wore, could say so

much about a man. The light grey crew-neck he had on picked up that silvery iridescent ring in his eyes, or—perhaps more likely—was that just a reflection of anger? There was no way she could convince herself that he was paying a friendly visit. The lightweight tweed jacket in a soft muted rust with a grey silk handkerchief, a shade or two darker than the sweater, spilling from the breast-pocket, the grey trousers, the black loafer shoes, calf-leather, buffed to a fine sheen—every detail, even to the lazy way he lounged in the doorway, his hand thrust so carelessly into the trouser pocket, might have been planned to show a man laid-back and at ease, to conceal the incisive intelligence and keen observation...

Except that these were qualities she knew too well ever to be deceived. And now she had no intention of... But, in spite of all her attempted bravado, she swallowed nervously, regretting the weakness which had diverted her momentarily, for she had never seen him so chillingly angry, never seen such distaste deeply etched on every feature.

The mouth was pressed in a single straight line, the eyebrows were pulled together, and the eyes... They were the most disturbing of all, looking at her with something very close to dislike. Even though she told herself that she didn't care—and she didn't, not in the least—there was something so wounding in such a silent unjustified attack that she had to struggle to hold back the tears that were stinging so painfully behind her eyes.

But what on earth was she doing? Suddenly, angrily, she came to her senses, castigating herself for so much emotional self-indulgence. Why was she allowing him to barge his way into her home? Allowing him to dictate, make her feel guilty and inadequate and a hundred other negative qualities which she resented so fiercely?

'Well?' she asked, with what she hoped he would recognise as impatience laced maybe with a touch of sarcasm. 'This is quite a surprise, but I don't imagine you came here simply for the pleasure of standing looking at me.'

Still he seemed to be in no hurry to speak, but when he did it was slowly, and with a harshness she had not previously heard in his voice—one of his ways, she had little doubt, of intimidating his adversaries in court. 'I'm looking...trying to convince myself...that you are the same girl.' She held her breath; it hurt to breathe. 'The one I knew...or thought I knew...in Oxford.'

Anguish struck at her; she felt as if the vital blood, life itself, was draining from her heart. It took great courage, all the determination she could summon, to thrust her weakness aside, substituting cynical condescension. 'I rather think we've been here before—if you remember?'

'Yes, I remember.' And if he sighed then—she thought she caught the very faint, weary sound of it—she put it down to boredom rather than regret of any sort. 'So...what happened? What changed you so much? Even when we met again I could see you were different. What I could never have guessed was just how deep, how profound those changes were.'

How could he ask such questions—he of all people? Didn't he know what had happened? Was it so very difficult to guess? *He* was what had happened to change her, and—— Swiftly she caught tight hold of her thoughts, spoke with a patient detachment which she hoped he would see as boredom. 'I simply cannot see where this is leading.' How *dared* he, when she was feeling so vulnerable, so utterly defenceless? How dared he bulldoze his way back into her life, just when she was trying so hard to cope...? She said, with a rather desperate glance and a hand thrown out towards the table in the window, 'I do have someone coming this evening, and——'

'That's obvious.' Somehow his glance, as well as taking in the table with two places set, looked through the open bedroom door at the clothes spread out on the bed. But why should every word he spoke be thrown at her like some dire accusation? 'A quiet dinner for two, is it? Well, you needn't worry—I certainly have no inclination to disturb you. But, even in these liberated times, most people find this kind of thing unacceptable.'

While her brain was busy with that, trying to follow some kind of thread, he raked his fingers through his hair, a distracted gesture which in different circumstances would have provoked a desire to comfort; but then he went on.

'I wish...with all my heart I wish we had never met up again. It would have been better to hold

on to at least some of my illusions.' Now he spoke
softly, as if to himself, so softly that afterwards,
reliving the scene, she wondered if she had mis-
understood completely. 'Then what at the time
was like a miracle would not have turned into the
present nightmare.'

'Just a minute.' She frowned, struggling to sort
out the confusion of words and emotions. There
was some implication she didn't understand,
wanted to have clarified . . .

'No, *you* wait a minute.' All at once he was
rough, as if control was slipping; the step towards her was threatening, the hands reaching
out towards her were bruising through the thin
material of her robe. 'Can't you see it yourself,
for God's sake? What about your parents? What
will they think when they find out?'

A tiny shake loosened the robe, making it slip
from one shoulder. The wide eyes staring up at
him were brilliant with misery, and even when
one hand was linked about her slender neck,
when the blood surged in her veins as his finger
trailed across her skin, traced the tender hollow
of her throat, even then she refused to give way
to her feelings, which were nothing other than
sheer weakness and produced anger—for anger
was so much more appropriate to the scene she
was being forced to enact.

'I haven't the faintest idea what you're talking
about.' Wrenching herself away before his touch
could go further, before it could undermine all
her resolve, she retied her robe with trembling
fingers, then raised her head to glare defiance.

'But, since it seems to be a time for dishing out home-truths, you have a damned nerve, I must say, coming here to my flat, without invitation, to let me know what you think of me, accusing me of heaven knows what and expressing your opinions on matters that have nothing in the world to do with you.'

'I think I have a right to express an opinion simply because of what we once were to each other.'

'Because you seduced me, you mean?' How the words did not stick in her throat she couldn't explain. He had only had to look at her, to touch her cheek, to smile at her in that warm and utterly seductive way... Yes, the word was very appropriate. When he had turned on the battery of charm, nothing on this earth could have stopped her.

'Is that how you remember it?' There was a strange note in his voice; she wouldn't have said it was sorrow, maybe just a touch of regret at how things had gone sour. Whatever, his tone was enough to bring the aching soreness back into her chest, a pain which stifled any wish she might have had to contradict her own words. In any event, the moment had passed and he was continuing. 'It isn't at all like that in my memory, but perhaps—who knows?—I'm the one who is self-deluded. There's no doubt I was older, and I know ours was the first relationship you'd had that meant so much... But I can see I was probably wrong, and certainly if I had had any idea what it would lead to...'

'What it would lead to'... Little else registered; the earlier words were submerged in a wave
of righteous indignation which suddenly overwhelmed her, causing her to quiver with anger...

'Lead to you thinking you had earned the
lifelong right to interfere in my life? Oh, God,
you sound so unbearably pompous.' Now that
her attack had begun she found the words flowing
on their own. 'You won't say why you've come;
you hint at this and that in the most insulting
way; you're kind enough to describe what I've
become—at least, the version of my life according to Patrick Cavour. But tell me, what have
you become since Oxford? Are you going to stand
there and tell me you've led such a chaste life
that you can afford to pass judgement on other
people? Are you going to tell me there hasn't been
a whole string of women, starting with Gillian
Place?'

Not pausing to allow him to answer, she went
on in full spate—she was finding the experience
almost liberating. 'And, since you have the im-
pertinence to bring my parents into it, do tell me,
what do your parents think of the life you lead?
Or is it only women who are expected to allow
themselves to be insulted by these questions?'

'At least,' he answered hotly, 'I leave married
women alone. I do credit myself with a certain
amount of sense.'

So intent had she been on her own line of
questioning, so relieved to feel in control of the
situation for once, that it took a few minutes for
Leigh to gather the import of his words, and

when she did she was heady with anger. 'This really is intolerable—incredible. What right do you have to jump to conclusions the way you do? And why do you choose always to put the worst construction on relationships? Do you get a kick out of that? Or is it just that it boosts your ego to feel superior?'

'I notice you're not denying anything.'

'I don't think there's much point when you so clearly have your mind made up, and besides——' she had to bank down a rising tide of hysteria '—it is none of your business.'

He nodded coldly, as if her words were some dire confession. 'Of course, I understand—in fact certain things are becoming increasingly obvious. I appreciate the need in certain circumstances to keep your nerve, to deny everything, and if you're clever enough you might even divert attention from the truth. For a limited period. I suppose, that first night in Paris, I might have guessed the way things were, but I didn't.' He sighed. 'Chances were I didn't want to see what was in front of my nose. Anyway, it's getting late now, Leigh. In a day or two I understand it will all be public knowledge.'

'What?' She frowned, trying to follow his words, then wearily admitted that these days they no longer spoke the same language. 'I'm afraid you're too devious for me. I'm no longer willing to make the effort to try to understand.' There was an inexpressible sadness in recognising how deep and wide the chasm separating them was. 'And now, if you don't mind...' She half turned, just resisting the temptation to reach out to a table for support—she refused to give him the satisfaction of knowing how close to collapse she was.

Now he was right behind her—with all her senses she knew that—so she had to force herself to turn, calmly but challengingly. She could see the rapid rise and fall of his chest, knew that if she placed her fingertips against the grey cashmere there would be clear confirmation of his fury. Not that there was any need, not with his teeth so tightly clenched, not with his eyes narrowed and looking at her as if he had murder in mind.

And while they stared at each other, his arm moved, as if he was ready to grab her again, but instead his hand caught the edge of the table, dislodging something. It could have been nothing of importance, since there was no sound of a crash, and nothing, so far as she was aware, fell on to the carpet.

But then he was bending down, picking something up, some scrap which was hidden in his palm as he straightened and they continued to stare. She could hear the echo of her heart pounding against her ribcage, was glad when he broke off the confrontation to replace a scrap of paper, a tiny card...

But instead of putting it down he raised it again, looked from the card to her face and back again, before reading aloud in that damning, sneering voice, 'Captain James Brereton, Royal Navy.' Disparagement was in the eyes now raised to hers. 'A friend of yours?' A multitude of ac-

cusations and implications lurked in the seemingly innocuous query, implications which
brought indignant colour flooding to her cheeks,
but doubtless he would see her guilt being
proclaimed.

'Do you mind?' It was an attempt at coolness
undermined by the flashing contempt in her eyes.
But the hand she held out for the card was steady
enough. She had found the bit of paper in a
pocket the other day, had meant to put it in the
waste-bin, and now slipped it into the pocket of
her dressing-gown.

'You haven't answered my question.'

'I'm not in the witness-box.'

'And I suppose you'll say you're not on oath
either?'

'Precisely.'

'Is he married, this captain in the Royal Navy?'

'I haven't the faintest idea if he's married or
not.' She couldn't even remember what the young
man looked like.

'Ah.' There was a wealth of innuendo in the
single word, and in the faintly bitter smile which
accompanied it. 'How very wise. That's one way
you can plead total ignorance.'

There was no way she would dignify such a
remark with an answer, so, trying to ignore her
own fevered pulses and to retain some remnants
of dignity, she reminded him once more, 'I did
say I was expecting a guest...'

'And I told you I have no intention of breaking
up your dinner *à deux* but...a last word. Re-

member, when the whole thing breaks about your ears, I warned you...'

'I promise you I shall try to do that.' She spoke slowly, as if to a young child. 'Even though I haven't the least idea what you're talking about, I shall try to remember I was warned. And that you were the one who gave the warning. You shall have all the credit. Is that what you want?' She had managed to adopt a tone of sickly sweetness, but at the last minute her voice wobbled dangerously. Frantically she gnawed at her lower lip as she tried to retain her crumbling control. 'Now please will you go?'

'And remember, you're old enough——' he might have been deaf for all the notice he took '—and obviously experienced enough, to know that married men, whatever their protestations, are seldom there when you need them. When the going gets tough, that's when they rediscover all the benefits of married life—the safety of it, the comfort. That's when they hurry back to their wives and children.'

'Get out.' There was nothing you could tell this man; his pigheadedness was so total that for a moment she forgot her misery. 'Get out of my house and out of my life.'

'Yes.' Now his calmness was a foil for her anger. 'I can see now I was wrong to come.' His laughter was self-deprecating. 'It's amazing, amusing too, how bruised pride can undermine the most level-headed man. Not that my relationship with you has ever been level-headed—mad, deranged might have been more apposite—

but that taunt...the suggestion that you were ashamed of that night we spent together in Paris... If it hadn't been for that, things could have been so very... Ah, well.'

He sighed, turned for the door, and stopped. 'I confess, Leigh, that was the bitterest cut of all. Especially in view of what I know now.' Firmly he strode through the hall and, barely aware of what she was doing, she followed, watched him place his hand on the doorknob.

'I'm speaking to you as a lawyer now, Leigh. Prepare yourself for a rough ride. Once they become public, these things are inevitably humiliating—matters are made public which should concern only two people, and of course the gossips won't let it die. So, you may find you're not as tough as you thought you were.'

He eased open the door. 'Already the Palais is buzzing with speculation, and it won't be long till the media are in there too. I wish I could do something to help, but I doubt if there's much anyone can do. If I had a desert island somewhere I'd be happy to lend it to you, but...' He smiled wanly, shrugged. 'I hope to God you find it all worth it in the end.' He tipped her chin upwards, looked down into her eyes for what could have been a lifetime. 'Goodbye.' The door closed behind him. 'My love.'

She dreamed she had heard him whisper those words as he disappeared, but that was sheer self-delusion and she had over-indulged in that for more years than she cared to admit.

It was then that she began to shiver, long, racking rigors which reminded her of her barely dry hair and scantily covered frame. But even when she had dressed and had turned the heating to boost she could not control her shaking.

She managed—just—to get through the meal with Jane, but her friend insisted on leaving early, after seeing her into bed with a hot-water bottle and a supply of aspirin.

'Now, you see you take things easy tomorrow,' Jane ordered before closing the bedroom door. 'This kind of flu clears quickly, as a rule, so long as you catch it early. And you promise you'll call me if you need any help tomorrow?'

But when she was alone, staring numbly into the darkness, Leigh knew that her symptoms had little to do with the flu virus; much more likely she was heading for a complete breakdown. After all, she thought hopelessly, it had been incubating for the last five years.

CHAPTER EIGHT

ESCAPE was much easier than Leigh would have guessed possible, a matter which in less fraught circumstances might have been the cause of some concern. She visited the doctor, who, obviously sensing the emotional tension simmering so dangerously just below the surface, agreed all too readily that his patient was suffering from nervous exhaustion. What was more surprising was that Kyle, far from trying to dissuade her, appeared totally divorced from the problems which her going away would engender.

'I'm sorry, Kyle, leaving you in the lurch like this, especially with Anna away, but I feel I must have a break.'

'What?' Her explanations might have passed him by. 'Sorry, Leigh, what did you say?'

His lack of interest struck at her, adding to her present low self-esteem, and brought the all too ready tears pricking again. 'Just, as I said, I'm going to have to take sick-leave. I'm...' Her voice wobbled.

'Oh.' For the first time he looked at her with recognition. 'Well, if you must, of course... How long did you say you're likely to be away?'

'I'm not sure.' Firmly she banished her basic inclination, determined to stick to generalities. This was not, *not* the moment to throw in the towel, to give up everything she had striven for over the years. Later on, when she was in a calmer frame of mind, then would be the time, if she decided, to hand in her resignation, to make up her mind that Europe was scarcely big enough to hold both her and Patrick Cavour. Time enough then to look for something else. North America, perhaps. Even the Antipodes would hardly be distant enough. Eventually she spoke again. 'At least two weeks.' And maybe even two months, she promised herself.

'That's all right, Leigh.' Kyle appeared to be pulling himself together. 'Besides, quite apart from sick-leave, you haven't had a holiday this year, and——' he looked at her more closely '——you *don't* look your usual assured self, I must say.'

'No.' Again she struggled with her threatening emotions. 'Well, if you agree... I'm on stand-by for a flight to Heathrow later today. But...are you sure you can manage on your own, Kyle? If you like, I could ring an agency before I go and——'

'No, don't do that. In fact, I've just decided that I'm going to close the office for a spell. Things are quiet this time of the year, and if they pile up, so what? You're not to worry. Promise.'

'Yes, I promise.' It was easy to do that when she had lost all interest—in her job, her employer, in the very fate of Europe. Even the fear of Kyle on the rampage through her immaculate filing system failed to move her.

'You'll let me know how things go?' Although he smiled faintly, there was no doubt it was an effort. 'I can't afford to lose you. You know it's you who keeps the whole thing together.'

'I'll let you know. As soon as I can.'

Her arrival back at the vicarage in Great Whencote, the place where she had been born, where she had spent the greater part of her life, coincided with the most perfect spell of late summer weather. It was all so peaceful and un-demanding that she knew her decision had been the right one. If there existed on the face of the earth a place where souls could be restored, then this corner of rural Gloucestershire must surely have been it.

'You do know your mother is coming home next week?' Her father, seeming for once to be aware of what was going on around him, crumbled the last morsel of bread on his plate then assiduously pressed it together with a few slivers of cheese into a pellet which was popped into his mouth.

'Next week?' Leigh raised her head in sur-prise, pushed her chair back from the well-scrubbed kitchen table. 'But I thought she had another month? At least, that's what I gathered from the last letter I had from her.'

'That was the plan, but——' David Gregory's smile was almost mischievous '—she almost hinted she was feeling homesick. Strange, isn't it?' His expression grew more sombre. 'All these years she has seemed to dislike living here. But maybe—who knows?—this spell apart might have been good for both of us. I know I've missed her, and I shall tell her so.'

'I should do,' she said gently. 'We all like to hear these things. Anyway, it does seem as if she's enjoyed herself, and the climate has obviously suited her.'

'Mmm. Well, that's another reason for hoping the weather holds for another week or two. It would be a pity if she were to come back to the chilly weather we had last month. Speaking of that, why not make the most of it and treat yourself to another spell in the hammock this afternoon? You look better already. You know, I was quite concerned about you when I met you at the station—so white and all eyes...'

'Mmm. I know.' Abruptly Leigh rose and began to collect the debris of their simple meal. 'Thought we'd got a panda to stay when I looked in the hall mirror. The after-effects of that virus I was telling you about. And I think I'll take you up on that—indulge myself while I can. There's nothing quite like settling down in the hammock with a good book, knowing perfectly well that you'll be drowsing before you reach the bottom of the page...'

'A wonderful feeling,' he agreed abstractedly as he picked up a newspaper and frowned over the crossword. 'I'm going to settle down in the study for an hour... Are you feeling inspired, Leigh? Perhaps you can solve this. It should be so easy, and it looks like "moped", but...

"Something for which the leg-weary cyclist pined." Why...'

'There is something called a mo-*ped*, Father.' Leigh smiled affectionately. 'It's a sort of under-age motorcycle.'

'Of course.' He shook his head reprovingly. 'It will surprise you to know that I have heard the word. I'll just go and get a pen...' As he crossed the hall she could hear him whistling tunelessly, while she, slowly drying a plate, glanced down at the folded newspaper, eyes searching for another clue... Mmm, that could be...possibly was... But that one... She was still puzzling over the second clue when a name jumped out at her from the small news items on the back page. She drew in a startled breath, her heart beginning to thump against her ribs as the significance of the words was absorbed.

'Mrs Kay Lessor, wife of MEP Mr Kyle Lessor, is seeking a divorce,' she read, her eyes wide with shock. She skimmed the brief news item and reached the implication in the last line. 'It is understood that Mrs Lessor intends to name a secretary, Miss Anna Craig, in her petition.'

No. She dropped on to a chair, raked a shaky hand through her hair. *No*. She couldn't believe it. Not Kyle. And more especially not Anna, not shy and slightly colourless Anna. Frowning, she shook her head. But if it should be true, how was it she had never guessed...?

The door was pushed open as her father reappeared, wandered over to the boiler, picked up his pipe, began to tap down the tobacco...

'Any luck, Leigh?'

'What?' Her eyes were without comprehension.

'Any more luck with the crossword?'

'No, I'm sorry...'

'Well, I'll take it with me, and if you want me I'll be in the study. As I said, you go out into the garden, get some colour back in your cheeks.' Even as he spoke he was on his way back to the study; she could hear him reading another clue under his breath.

Still in shock, and without being completely aware of what she was doing, she picked up her book and drifted down to the far end of the garden to where the hammock was suspended. She remembered it being there from way back in the days of her early childhood, between the two ancient apple trees always jokingly referred to as the orchard. She swung herself into it and lay back, one long bare leg allowed to droop over the side, a disregarded sandal slipping from her slender foot as she adjusted the pillow to support her head.

Kyle...well, on reflection she could just about understand it of him, but *Anna*. How completely out of character it seemed, and yet... Pondering, she lay back, contemplating the patches of blue sky chequered with leaves. A few bees buzzed lazily about a clump of daisies and a butterfly settled momentarily on her hand, fluttering away as she reached out for her book. And as her mind went chasing round in circles various tiny clues and signs which had lodged at the back of her mind began to click into place, to make sense. But, although it was on Kyle and Anna that she was determined to concentrate, her brain would have none of it. It was Patrick Cavour who was there in front of her, so dominating, so accusing. And for the first time she knew what he had meant.

She drew in several shuddering breaths, blinked once or twice to clear a persistent film about her eyes, then, with some deliberation, pressed her lips together, closed her eyes and willed herself, with every ounce of strength she could summon, to relax. Starting at her head, working right down to her toes.

This, then, was what it was all about—the hints and innuendo. All the time Patrick had been accusing her of an affair with her boss. With Kyle, for heaven's sake. She gave a tiny scoffing laugh which very nearly translated into a sob. Kyle Lessor who *had*, it was true, propositioned her in her first month in Strasbourg, but who had at least taken her refusal with grace, had never mentioned the subject again, and who had, for all she knew, gone on immediately to someone else.

Kyle. But surely Patrick must have realised that she knew and was friendly with Kay Lessor? Did he think she was the kind of woman who...? She struggled to bring things down to earth from the high emotional plane which could wreak such havoc. Besides, apart from anything else, Kyle was half a head shorter than she was, and...

Oh, God. If only he had come out with it all there and then instead of so many hints and evasions... In spite of all her resolve, she felt tears on her cheek, reached into the pocket of her brief skirt, found she was without a handkerchief then used the hem of her faded T-shirt to dry her face.

She would not, *would not* think about it any more. She had wasted too many years of her life already. She would ignore the persistent and uncomfortable pressure in her chest and read a few pages of her novel... Sniffing, she opened the book at the marked page, tried to concentrate on the text instead of her own stupid feelings, read a few lines...

Then, with a weary, defeated sigh, she put the book aside. Later, there would be plenty of time. She leaned the side of her face against the softness of the cushion, allowed her eyelids to droop. She felt so indescribably weary, so hopeless... At last her breathing calmed... her lashes lay like tiny fragile fans against her creamy, sun-dappled skin...

Slowly the idyllic afternoon wore on and she began to slide away, blissfully away, from all the anguish of reality, drifting in and out of sleep without opening her eyes, only vaguely aware of the subtle changes of light, of lengthening shadows and a slight easing of the exhausting heat of earlier on in the day. In the comfort of lying there, so quiet and undisturbed, it was almost possible to switch off from what had happened, to blot from her mind all Patrick's bitter, incomprehensible accusations...

A sudden twist of pain in her stomach contradicted her; she murmured a protest as she tried to push away the recent hurtful memories. Even that long-ago agony had been nothing to compare with this, she admitted to herself.

'Can you forgive me, Leigh?' His voice was so close, so *real*, despite being all in her head. So real, so precious and yet so unutterably sad. There was no way she could refuse, or want to, especially here, where all things were possible.

'Of course.' Her lips moved with the thought. 'Of course I can forgive.' For she had learned the hard way about forgiveness. All those years of regret—what comfort had they offered...? Her heart leapt in her breast as a hand touched her, circling the foot dangling so invitingly over the side of the hammock, as fingers curved over the tender skin of her instep, impossibly arousing... In her veins an irresistible tingling rose. She wanted to retreat into dreams, where it was safe, but something stroked delicately, and the impossibly long, incredibly dark lashes swept back. And she forgot to breathe.

For a long time neither of them spoke, she from fear that the vision would evaporate with the same stealth of its arrival, and he—who knew?—possibly because at that moment to look was enough; that was what the dark eyes hinted, with their searching warmth. And maybe it was the intensity of his regard which reminded her of how she must look. One hand rose in an effort

to restrain the tumble of untidy hair, then her
fingers trailed apologetically across a face devoid
of make-up, and panic set in as she recalled her
none too clean shirt and her skirt, which was a
left-over from her schooldays. She must get up
and try to...

'No.' A firm hand restrained her. 'No, don't
move. Please. I just want to look...'

'Patrick.' Her breath was released in a tor-
mented sigh. 'For a moment I thought...you
weren't really there, that I was seeing things.'

'And...' still his eyes refused to move from
her face, from her mouth '...what did you hope?
That you would blink once and find I had gone,
replaced by a frog, perhaps?' He smiled bleakly.

'No—I don't know.' Feverishly she bit her lip.
'At least...'

'Tell me.' When he spoke like that, command-
ingly, imperiously, it was impossible to refuse.
'Tell me what you felt.' His fingers were still
about her foot, moving almost imperceptibly
against that tender skin with totally devastating
effect.

'Surprised, you could say. Even shocked.' Her
shoulders moved under the thin cotton.
'And——' she forced her eyes from his, sight-
lessly looking across the wide meadow which
surrounded the garden '—I don't want any
more...confrontation, Patrick.' For a moment,
faced with loss of control, she gnawed at her
lower lip, then, finding some remnants of
courage, she faced him again. 'I can't take any
more of that. I've had enough to last me forever

and I've come back here to get over it. To *try* to get over it.' Her manner was weighty with misery.

He frowned, shook his head briefly. 'Everything you say, every reproach, I deserve. But, as to confrontation, I too hope that's all in the past.'

'Then...' In some strange way she was detached, in a sort of limbo, hovering halfway between inexpressible joy and utmost despair—to neither of which, she determined, she would give way. But, strangely, something of the recent anguish had eased; it was enough for the time being that he was here with her, that she was looking into his eyes and seeing neither indictment nor damnation. It was very much like the dream, that perfect reprieve from much of the awful abrasiveness of reality...

'Can you forgive me, Leigh?' Now that he was no longer touching her foot she felt insecure. 'I did ask a moment ago, and thought you said you would. Did I imagine it, I wonder?'

'Forgive?' Her voice, her eyes grew dreamy; she felt they had been here before, then remembered the reception and the same question. It had all started again from there.

'You want your pound of flesh?' The firm mouth curved slightly. 'I can't say I blame you. I'm not used to apologies, Leigh, but then neither am I used to making such a complete fool of myself. As a lawyer, I should be extremely sceptical of circumstantial evidence, so it's quite humbling to realise how I could have jumped to so many idiotic conclusions.'

He shrugged, raised his hands and looked about him for a moment, before returning all his attention to her. 'Here, in the garden of a country vicarage, I ask myself how I could have done it—it seems impossible that I reached the conclusions I did. Put it down...' He paused, his eyes searching her features with a flaying intensity which made her quiver. 'Put it down to... quite insane jealousy.'

The blood drained from her head then, her mind a surging confusion of thoughts and fears. That this man, this man above anyone, should think, should have imagined... A sob forced its way from her throat, a tear slid from the corner of her eye and down her cheek. And yet... Jealousy? The insane kind? There was a perversity here; there was intense pain yet a stirring hope...

'Leigh, don't.' The anguish in his voice was something with which she could identify and sympathise. 'For God's sake don't. I can't bear it if I make things worse for you.' A distracted hand raked through the dark hair. 'Sooner than that I would go away now, leave you in peace and never interfere in your life again. I can't begin to understand how I could have believed... you and Kyle...'

'And that other one.' Reminding him was irresistible; even as she spoke she felt the healing process begin, helped, perhaps, by the touch of self-derision. 'Don't forget you accused me of an affair with that naval man——' his name refused to come to mind at the moment '—simply on the grounds that he was married—or so you believed.'

'Well!' He had the grace to look embarrassed. 'You remember, I explained—I was half out of my mind with jealousy. Seeing you, all cool perfection, telling me it was not my business—and I knew that already—imagining you with them... It didn't matter that I had no rights; that had no effect on my feelings. I just hated the thought of you with either of them.' His laugh had a bitter note. 'Or with anyone, come to that.' Turning away, he leaned against the tree close to her. 'I suppose, even if... the man in your life, the one you told me about, if he turns out to be the most eligible man in the whole of Europe, it will make no difference. I'll hate him with all the passion I devoted to Kyle Lessor.'

'What?' Things were moving too quickly for her...

'Yes.' He laughed briefly. 'Sounds crazy, doesn't it? I surprised myself with the strength of my feelings. I had always thought of myself as a fairly rational man but the last few weeks have made me revise that opinion. Possibly that's not a bad thing for a lawyer—we ought to be aware that, even in the most ordered lives, something can happen to knock you completely off-course.'

It was as if her brain had jammed in neutral; she couldn't seem to get on to his wavelength. 'I'm still trying to decide what on earth you're saying. Is it... is it something to do with James Brereton?' Then, when his face took on the blankness that she herself was experiencing, it seemed the ideal moment to seize her chance. 'The naval officer? The one you added to my list of... lovers?' she accused him innocently.

'Oh, that.' His expression was one of shame-faced guilt. 'Well, I suppose I ought to expect you to pile on the agony, and I'm not complaining, don't think that, but as to the special man in your life, you were quite open about it when I came to your flat that day.' A faint narrowing of her eyes indicated increased watchfulness, and he saw colour come and go in her face. 'Is it so painful for you to discuss it? "Ashamed" was the word you used at the time. I remember it well,' he added, with a faint smile which did little to conceal his bitterness.

'Neither of those things.' Now she was beginning to understand what had previously been so confused, but it was vital to damp down the wilder excesses of hope and expectation which she felt bubbling up. But everything he had said, every word uttered, did seem to point in one direction. Nevertheless, she determined to exercise great control in her reply—already there had been too many misunderstandings. Take your time, she told herself; don't rush. But, unable to trust herself, she concentrated her attention on the book in her hand, sliding a finger once or twice along the length of the glossy spine.

Lying here, so close to him, her heart hammering with wild, exultant strokes, she knew with total certainty that she wanted this man, longed for him with all the urgency of a passionate

nature. It didn't matter if there had been a dozen
Gillian Places; the past was over and nothing was
going to stop her reaching out and seizing what
she wanted. She would use all the skill and guile
and determination of a man-eater if that was
what it took. She had had time to study methods
recently; now she decided to hunt with the best
of them.

'And,' he prompted at last, invading her
thoughts, 'if neither applies, then what?'

'Oh...' A sudden loss of control defeated all
the easy resolve of a moment before; words
tumbled out without consideration. 'I'm lying—
of course I am.' The eyes she raised to his were
darkly brilliant, sparkling with insecure tears. 'I
find it both painful and shaming, but not——'
feverishly she caught at her lip '—not exactly for
the reasons I gave you then. Maybe——' she
choked on a shaky smile '—maybe it's time for
me to ask *you* to forgive...'

'Go on.' If she had been less involved in her
own emotions, less troubled by the tremors
caused by his oh, so persuasive tones, she might
have seen that he too was finding control less than
easy, that his hands were clenched to stop him
reaching out. 'Go on, Leigh.' This was the skilled
advocate at his most seductive. 'I know you can't
have done anything so terrible, anything that
needs forgiveness...'

'That day in Paris...after...after...' Hot
colour stained her face. 'When you followed me.'
Regaining control now, she spoke with an appearance of detachment. 'When I said I was in-

volved with someone else, it wasn't true. There was no one else. Not that it seemed to matter, since you were all too ready to believe——'

'And why did I believe, Leigh?' He raked a hand through his hair, spoke through his teeth. 'Ask yourself that, for God's sake.' For what seemed a lifetime they stared at each other, then she saw him close his eyes, press a clenched fist to his forehead as if determined to force comprehension. 'But why in heaven's name did you lie about it? That's what I can't understand.'

It was a moment before she answered, searching for the right words for herself as much as for him. 'I suppose it was mostly that I wanted to pay you back. For Oxford. For the years in between and . . .' She faltered, struck by the idea that so much spontaneous self-examination might be unwise. There was little doubt that it contradicted all her decisions of a moment before. 'And, even more than that, perhaps—*perhaps*,' she emphasised, as if she too was questioning her reasons, 'it had something to do with pride.

'You see——' she drew in one deep, shuddering breath, then looked at him with something like accusation '—I had convinced myself that I was safe, in complete charge of my own destiny, that never again would any man—not just you,' she threw in almost apologetically, 'snap his fingers and——' the tip of her tongue passed over her lips '—and then I'd wake up in his bed. I thought I was so strong, so much in control of my life, and then to find . . . Here I was, twenty-five years old, so much more experienced and yet making the same elementary mistakes I had made when I was a student. Surely you can see that that was enough to make anyone feel ashamed?' Searching his face, she waited for a reply, and when he said nothing, just stood there looking down at her, she grew all nervous and jumpy again. 'Well, can't you?'

'Experienced?' It was exasperating that he should ignore most of what she had said and pick up on a single indiscreet word. 'That's what you said just now, and it could mean such a lot or it could mean nothing at all...'

Anger shook her. Men could be so transparent, and she resented being questioned on this subject just as much as she had the last time it had come up. 'If you're asking about my sex-life, then don't. *Don't*,' she insisted as he seemed about to speak, and somehow, even lying there, she gave the impression that if she had been standing on her feet one of them would have been stamped. 'Not unless and until you are prepared for me to do likewise. I very much doubt if *your* life has been entirely chaste since Oxford and——'

'Almost.'

'And,' she raced on, without the word having registered, 'once we've established that, then maybe we can compare lists and——' Suddenly she stopped, her wide violet eyes searching his with suspicion. 'What? What did you say?'

'I said, almost.' His tone was aggravatingly patient, maybe even a little smug. 'You implied a question and I answered it. And, before we go on, may I say that more than anything I regret that I can't give a different answer? I would like to say "entirely" but...'

She stared, her normally sharp brain like some ancient rusting machine, but if she was right he seemed to be saying... 'But——' it was close to a wail, and she missed the flicker of a smile caused by her reaction '—you've lived in California.'

'Washington,' he corrected her. 'And can I say, in defence of a country I love, that it's not all sex and drugs, in spite of the images you see? Not everyone in the States lives like a tomcat. Not even the women,' he added wryly.

'Oh.' It was hard to know what to say.

'And am I right in thinking that in exchange for that information you offered a quid pro quo? Some people in the profession call it plea bargaining.'

She looked at him with suspicion. He was altogether too bland, was now giving the impression of being wholly in control, but she *had* indicated, foolishly as it turned out... She averted her head, conscious that her earlier confidence and euphoria were ebbing fast. There was little doubt that it was shaming in these liberated times. He would think no one had been interested enough to...

'I've had only one partner in my life.' Accusingly, she faced him. 'Ever,' she added, to avoid future misunderstandings.

'Leigh.' That voice, so soft, so tender, was almost an encouragement to tears, but she

wouldn't risk a deluge even if it did wipe away
the miseries of the past years, and in any case his
outstretched hand stifled that inclination,
tangling in her hair, delicately tracing the line of
her cheek, curving about the nape of her neck.

'What fools.' As he smiled he shook his head
despairingly. 'What fools we are. Me for jumping
so readily to conclusions, and you——' he gave
her a reproving little shake '—you for baling out
as you did that morning in Paris. When we woke
up together I meant to...' He grinned mischie-
vously. 'At least, the *second* thing I meant to do
was to put something to you, a proposition, a
pro——'

'Oh, Patrick.' Her life was all at once a dazzling, blinding prospect; joy was exploding inside
her, taking her straight up to the stratosphere. 'I
think I know.' With just a touch of shyness she
reached out for his free hand, rubbed gently at
the inner skin of his wrist. 'You want us to go
back to how things were in Oxford; you're asking
me to come and live——'

'No.' His denial was so fierce that her eyelids
flicked back in apprehension. His expression was
so serious that the bubbles of pleasure burst, and
she was dropping to earth so fast that she was
bound to hit rock-bottom with a crippling crash.
'No,' he repeated less fiercely. 'There can't be any
going back for us. That is the very last thing in
the world I want.'

CHAPTER NINE

LIGHT-YEARS might have passed as they stared at each other, though in fact it was seconds. Leigh, wide-eyed, desperate, felt her mouth tremble, and pressed her lips together, determined that Patrick would never guess how she felt. Even though he was looking at her with such intensity that he must be planning to say they must part forever.

'Oh ... I see.' Her tone of vague interest was masterly.

'Leigh.' It was a weary and in the end almost a reproving sigh. 'What on earth are you thinking? Oh, I suppose it's my fault again. I'm making such a muck-up of all this.' His hand was trailing down her cheek again, and he could have no idea of the effect of his thumb brushing once or twice against her trembling mouth. 'What I'm saying is, I don't want us to live together—at least, not *just* live together.'

Emotions were building inside her; she was holding her breath in superstitious fear of damaging the fragile hopes and aspirations that his words were stimulating; it was dangerous to allow herself to believe ...

'Leigh, my darling.' She breathed again, all the stony fears inside her seeming to ease and shift. 'Five years ago it was a terrible error not to make a commitment, not to ask you to make one. I suppose . . .' He shrugged, smiled down at her in a regretful kind of way. 'I suppose the commitment was taken for granted, but I'm not going to repeat the same mistakes. This time there's got to be more to it. It's not just a question of slipping into bed with you, though God knows that's on my mind most of the time. No, I want it to be permanent, acknowledged by the whole world. I want you, in time, to have my children.

'So I'm afraid this time it's marriage, Leigh. Could you bear it, do you think?' He gave, she thought, little indication that he had doubts about her answer, looking down at her with typical Cavour confidence.

'For us to be married at the very earliest date it can be arranged? Tomorrow wouldn't be too soon for me.'

'Oh.' For a moment she seemed about to weep. 'Oh, *Patrick*!' There was accusation in both her tone and manner.

'Leigh?' His voice held perhaps just a shade of uncertainty.

'Patrick Cavour, how could you do it? How could you ask me to marry you when I'm wearing this . . . this disgusting old T-shirt and a skirt I've had since I was seventeen, while you. . . ?' Quickly she took in his casual dark trousers, the checked shirt with sleeves folded back to display strong brown forearms, the dark green tie, highly polished shoes—he was always so immaculate. '*You*.' She gestured with one outflung arm.

'Oh.' He laughed then, and gave her a little shake. 'If it will make you happy then I'll go and look out my sackcloth and ashes, but not before you give me my answer, put me out of my misery and tell me you'll marry me.'

'Try to stop me.' This time she put her arms about his neck and pulled his face down to hers. 'Just try. Of course I'll marry you. I love you and simply have no choice in the matter. But still, I would have preferred it if you'd chosen a moment when I was wearing something glamorous. Or even something slightly less revolting.'

'To me you look beautiful no matter what you're wearing. And the important thing is that you're wearing *something*.' His mouth moved with tantalising slowness against hers.

'Oh?' What on earth could he mean?

'That day—night, rather—in Paris, I woke in the early hours and almost woke you up to ask you—to tell you, rather—that you must marry me. But then I realised how inappropriate it would be to propose to you when we were in bed together, and besides, you looked so deeply, so innocently asleep...

'Now look—if you keep doing that——' he caught at her hands, nibbled reprovingly at her fingers '—we'll be back in a similar and inappropriate situation, and I've never fancied making love in a hammock. Besides which——' he glanced up at the branch supporting the top end '—I very much doubt if this tree is capable of supporting our joint weights, and I don't want to appear at our wedding on crutches or pushing a zimmer frame. And, apart from that, there's always the chance of a surprise visit from your father, and I don't want him to draw any wrong conclusions when I ask him to marry us next week.'

Leigh giggled. 'Oh...Father. I almost forgot about him. Tell me, what did he say when you appeared?'

'I think he was...slightly surprised, shall I say?...by my desperate request to see you. In fact, I half expected him to slam the door and ring the police.'

'Idiot.'

'But he remained perfectly calm and told me where I could find you. Oh...and he did say he remembered me—picked me out from your large gallery of admirers.'

'Mmm, he does have a tremendous memory.' Then, as his hands tightened about her waist, she relented, with an abrupt change of subject. 'When you said as soon as possible, Patrick— for the wedding, I mean—how soon is soon?'

'Tomorrow?' he said hopefully, then smiled at the determined shake of her head. He compromised. 'Next week?'

'Impossible. My mother is due back from New Zealand next week. We couldn't possibly...'

'Ah, yes. Of course we couldn't. I want everyone to be happy for us and with us. But I do mean to set a time limit.'

'Do you, indeed?'

'I do. A five-year wait is enough for the most patient man. But tell me, you've never been to the States, have you?' She shook her head without speaking, the expression in her luminous eyes saying more than words ever could. 'I do have to go to New York in three weeks. If we could arrange things before then we could go together, and I know the most perfect little cottage in Vermont where we could be completely alone and——'

'Three weeks?' She shook her head in total if regretful dismissal of his idea. Men were so impatient, with no idea of what was involved in arranging these things. 'It's just impossible, Patrick. It wouldn't be the kind of wedding your family or mine would expect...'

'It's our wedding, yours and mine, not our families'. What we want is important too. The other things are peripheral. We needn't send out invitations—just ring our friends and tell them about the time and place. You can go out and buy a dress, I'll order cases of champagne and lots of caviare, and——'

'I'm sure your brothers would be thrilled to be offered little biscuits and blobs of caviare. I do remember they all had pretty healthy appetites. Besides, I loathe caviare.' She uncoiled herself at last from the hammock, stood up, and slipped her arms about his neck. 'You know...' she wriggled in pleasure as his hands spread across her back, pulling her possessively close '...you are quite, quite crazy.'

But the breathless accusation was stifled as his mouth covered hers, and it was some considerable time before he answered.

'I am,' he agreed, 'quite crazy for you. Always have been. And tell you what——' the teasing look reminded her that she had laughter to look forward to as well as all the tender, sensual joys '—if you care to go and put on the ballgown you wore at the reception, I'll take you out for dinner and propose all over again, and you can go faint with the shock of it all. That's how I had it all planned, that night in Paris when I lay in the dark beside you.'

'Quite, quite mad,' she said regretfully. 'You do remember that I flew home from Strasbourg and why? It was to recover from a broken heart, and I certainly did not visualise any occasion for wearing that very elaborate dress. I didn't plan to trail round the vicarage, acting Miss Havisham.'

'What you're saying is that the dress is still in your flat?'

'Exactly. But I do have a fairly presentable cotton dress I've worn just once.'

'I'm not so sure I'll fancy you in that, not when I'd set my heart on that blue one with the jazzy little bolero. You know, I felt completely knocked out when you turned round that night. I couldn't believe it at first; I thought I must be in the middle of a hallucination. I even liked that mad hairdo you had then. Maybe,' he hazarded, 'you could wear both for our wedding? It would save you the trouble of buying another dress.'

'No.' She shook her head definitely. 'I don't think so. It'll have to be something off the peg, but it's going to be completely traditional. Not white, perhaps, but——' her face had a dreamy look '—cream. Or ivory. I suppose even those aren't entirely appropriate, but...no one will know except us that I'm not...'

'Shh.' Frowning, he put his fingers over her lips. 'You are. Of course you are. More than any other woman I know. And if it helps to ease your conscience, for everyone's sake I think we should agree—and you must know it's the last thing in the world I want—that it would be best if we made up our minds to be extremely...decorous till the knot is tied.'

She giggled and caught at his hands. 'Well, if you would stop doing *that*, we might have a chance.' A vibrant, breathless smile was directed towards him. 'And something else—it might be a good idea if we went and told Dad our news, see which days are available for the wedding. And I think we ought to forget about going out to dinner. I made a perfectly reasonable casserole which we can have, and besides, I think we ought to start ringing round. I must contact Mum in New Zealand and you'll have to let them all know in Loughskerrie.' Her expression changed, grew a little more serious. 'I wonder what they'll think of it all?'

'What they'll think I can tell you right now: What took you so long? That's what they'll want to know. They still ask about you from time to time, and Fergal, when he wants to be particularly awkward, tells me I was a fool to let you slip through my fingers.'

'I hope you're telling me the truth, but come *on*.' Taking his hand, she began to pull him towards the house. 'Dad must be dying with curiosity. Oh, I think maybe it's going to be *fun* getting ready in such a rush—only hope Mum agrees with me. Oh, Patrick.' Suddenly she stopped, turned to him, her expression thoughtful. 'Thank you. For turning my life round in this fantastic way. I'm still half inclined to think I'm in a dream. An hour or two ago I was so utterly miserable and then you appeared. It's magic.'

'Leigh.' His hand smoothed her hair, then held her head against his chest. 'I wish I could wipe out all the misery. But with all my heart——' now the deep voice was deliberately lighter '—I promise to do better for the rest of our lives.'

'You'd better.' Infected by the threatened laughter, she raised her head to study his face. 'Positively no more Gillian Places. You do realise that, I hope?'

'Ah, yes.' He frowned. 'Now, there's a name you mentioned once before, though at the time I couldn't place it. It was just the other day I remembered. She was a nurse, I think, who was at one time down to join the group for Ashala, but in the end she was transferred to another project—in South India, I think. I heard she married one of the doctors there.'

'But...' Anguish stabbed at Leigh as she reflected on the effect of that name through the years. 'I thought...' Abruptly she stopped, reassessing things in her mind.

'Yes?' he prompted. 'You thought? What did you think, Leigh?'

'One day, in Oxford, I met Debbie Fleetham. You won't deny you knew her, I suppose?' she asked a little waspishly.

'No, I'd be crazy to deny that.' He spoke so reasonably that she felt ashamed.

'I wasn't accusing you,' she said, with so little truth that they both grinned and he raised a questioning eyebrow. 'Well, maybe just a little. You see, I've always been wildly jealous of Gillian Place ever since...'

'You had no need. But you were saying you met Debbie Fleetham one day...'

'And she told me...' Frowning, she tried to recall the exact wording used. '"She——" Gillian Place, that was "—she's off to Bangladesh with Patrick Cavour; they must be in New York by this time." Oh, and she said something about it being romantic.'

'And you *believed* her?'

'Yes.' Now even she could hardly understand why she had been so credulous. 'I suppose at the time I was vulnerable, not entirely logical.'

'Yes, well, I know the feeling.' He sighed. 'As far as Gillian Place is concerned I think she might have been on the same flight, but I couldn't be sure. I don't think I can even put a name to the face. Or vice versa.'

'A beautiful blonde with a stunning figure, according to Debbie,' she put in helpfully.

'Ah, but there were so many answering to that description.'

'So long,' she replied to his teasing, 'as there are none in the future.'

'Anyway, Debbie was most likely just showing
her claws. Remember I told you we went out once
or twice in a group? Before her birthday party...'

'Yes, you did tell me that. I suppose it should
have occurred to me at the time that she was most
likely a bit jealous.'

'Ah, well, we all know about that, don't we?
But, while we're on the subject, there have to be
no more intimate dinners with roués like your
employer.'

'Intimate, did you say? Fat chance of that with
you around, but, in any case, it was entirely platonic, as I've told you several times.'

'Yes, it looked like it from where I was standing
on the river-walk—the two of you locked in a
close embrace.'

'I promise it wasn't the least bit like that. He
was comforting me because he could see I was
so miserable after——'

'Comforting himself quite a lot, I should say.'

'After seeing you with Inés da Silva,' she said
reprovingly.

'Ah, yes. Inés. And did he know why he was
comforting you?'

'I didn't tell him, but he might have guessed.
I imagine the vibes were pretty strong that night,
and we know he is a very sensitive man.' She
spoke sardonically. 'Anyway, he was particularly
sweet; he knew I was unhappy and did his best
to help. I hope you notice that I'm not the least
bit curious about your date with Inés.'

'Who might just turn out to be a relative of
mine.' He was poker-faced.

'Tell me another,' she scoffed.

'As I was about to say, when I first met Iné
at the reception—the one where you treated m
with such disdain...' When she giggled he pause
dramatically, then continued. 'While you pre
tended to have difficulty placing me in your lon
list of lovers, Inés, on the other hand, was ver
interested in my——'

'I bet she was.'

'*Must* you keep interrupting? Now I re
member it always was one of your more irritatin
habits. No, don't do that.' He caught the fis
which had been aiming for his chin. '*Don't* d
that,' he repeated, and they stared intently at eac
other for a moment, eyes sparkling. 'Not,' h
warned, 'unless you're prepared to take the con
sequences. Interested in my name, I was abou
to say.' Suddenly his composure cracked, he wa
grinning, and a moment later they were bot
laughing helplessly.

'Your...your name?'

'Apparently her mother is a Cavour, and the
trace their family back to the *conquistadores*
so...'

Leigh made a great show of treating the matte
seriously. 'So there's quite a chance that it wa
one of her family who set off in 1588, missed h
way and ended up in Loughskerrie?'

'More than likely, I should say.' He grinne
and instantly they were both shaking wit
laughter again, both revelling in the amiabl
light-hearted sparring which had added such spi
to their relationship from the beginning.

With an effort Leigh concentrated on what he was saying. 'She's a very attractive woman, Inés, f——'

'Oh, yes, a lot of men have thought so.'

'If you like that type, but I've always preferred a more willowy shape...'

'Tell me, Patrick——' it seemed appropriate to ask, when she was so warmly gathered against him '—did you have any idea when you came to Strasbourg that I was——?'

'Not the slightest.' He was so definite that she knew she had been fooling herself from the beginning. 'But I think that, quite without knowing it, I had been looking out for you over the years—searching rooms when I went to parties, looking up expectantly when I heard a certain type of voice. Deep down I don't think I ever accepted that we wouldn't meet again, but I lost contact with most of our friends when I was in Ashala, and besides, I convinced myself that you would have married by this time, and I had no intention of rocking the boat for you.'

'Oh.' Such a carbon copy of her own experience was hardly surprising...

'Tell you what, though.' Twisting round in his arms, she observed his slightly guilty expression as he spoke. 'I do have one confession.' Her raised eyebrow encouraged him to continue. 'The flight that day to Paris—it wasn't entire coincidence. I met Kyle in the corridor and something he said gave me a clue. From there it wasn't difficult to discover which flight you were on. And yes, I did persuade the girl at the check-in desk

to arrange for me to have the seat next to you
Though for all the good it did me... You wer
quite unspeakable.'

She giggled, and blushed with as much coynes
as a fulsome compliment might have produced
'I was, wasn't I? But you flirted outrageousl
with the stewardess so you deserved it.'

'And you dismissed my invitation to dinner a
if I had the plague. And then,' he remembere
with indignation, 'as I was getting out of the lif
I met Kyle on his way up to your room. And no
you're surprised that I drew certain conclusions!

'I was and I am.' Standing on tiptoe, she spok
with her mouth against his. 'But, since you apol
ogised for all your unfair accusations, I've mad
up my mind to forgive you for causing me s
much pain. Besides, you weren't to know that h
had Anna hidden discreetly away in his taxi-cab

'Magnanimous of you, I'm sure. B
now——' he frowned '—I suppose there are on
or two things we ought to sort out. Your flat, fo
one. I suppose you'll want to go over t
Strasbourg and collect your things and——?'

'Either that,' she put in innocently, 'or yo
could give up yours. It's perfectly possible t
commute daily to Paris.'

'Is it?' There was the faintest of smiles on h
face as he looked down at her. 'The problem i
a lot of my work means travelling world-wide
and I expect whenever possible that you shoul
go with me—in the early days at least.' H
meaning was so clear that she felt herself gro

warm, and deliberately looked down to hide the evidence.

'But... I did think I might just hang on to my job for a bit. After all, most people do these days.'

'No chance.' That was categoric enough. 'I haven't found you again simply to settle for an arm's-length marriage. I'm earning enough to keep us both in reasonable comfort, and if you do find you have time on your hands there will be plenty of organisations who will jump at the chance of using your skills.'

'So...it's come to this. I'm to give up my tinpot job in favour of ironing your shirts...'

'A much more worthwhile occupation.' He grinned and it was impossible for her to stop her own mouth curving in response. 'You know what I think of most politicians. And I can see——' now there was a speculative expression in his dark eyes '—that that expression still rankles...'

'It does.' She aimed a playful punch at his shoulder, frowned when he grimaced as if in pain. But it rankled even more when I discovered just how futile it all was. You know, I never did discover what happened to all the immaculate reports I produced for them. Went in the shredder, I expect.'

'My poor darling. What a depressing experience for your first job.' He kissed the tip of her nose. 'How much more satisfying if you had come with me to Ashala. Teaching basic hygiene and helping to care for abandoned children might not have had the same cachet but, I promise you, it would have been much more worthwhile. Be sides which, we would have been together.'

'Yes.' A shadow crossed her face. 'Yes, and to think that if it hadn't been for that chance meeting with Debbie Fleetham I would have fol lowed you. I had decided to swallow my pride and ask you to find a place for me...'

'Pride.' He sighed, and his arms tightened about her. 'I had more than my share too. I should have carried you off by force when you didn't agree to come voluntarily. I would do that now if you were to show any sign of changing your mind, so...'

'As I think I told you, no chance.' She laid her head on his chest, but almost immediately began to detach herself. 'Heavens.' She was blushing again. 'I just caught sight of Dad at the kitchen window. I keep forgetting about him, but we'd better go and tell him. I only hope the shock isn't too much for him.'

But when they went into the kitchen, eyes glowing, fingers entwined, though he went through all the familiar expressions of surprise and pleasure, Leigh had the impression that the news was not quite the bombshell they had anticipated.

CHAPTER TEN

WHEN she reached the lych-gate of the Norman church and found it barred, the bride paused, exhibiting mock-dismay, then smiled appealingly to the children enacting the old tradition. But it was only after coins had changed hands that the seven-year-old girl began to untie the gate. 'Thank you, Caroline.' Leigh paused, knowing the girl would be anxious afterwards to give a detailed report of the dress, and besides, she had known her all of her life.

'You look just...lovely, Leigh.' The child spoke shyly, while the others murmured agreement.

'And that's a remark I have to agree with.' Her father waited as she gathered up the skirt of her gown and stepped on to the flagged path curving through the churchyard towards the porch. 'I think I'm safe to say I've never seen a prettier bride.'

'Not that you're at all biased,' she teased gently to hide her emotions. 'I bet every father who has walked up here with his daughter has said the very same thing.' She gave his arm a tiny squeeze, which in its quiet way was an acknowledgement of the shift in their relationship. 'Not that I'm complaining, and ... I'm glad you're giving me away. It wouldn't have felt right going up the aisle on someone else's arm.'

'Well, the archdeacon adds something which a mere parish priest cannot, and when he's your godfather as well... And you do know how pleased we are, your mother and I, that you're marrying Patrick, don't you? You seem so right for each other. In fact, we thought that the first time you brought him to meet us, quite a long time ago. We expected wedding-bells right then, but I suppose...you were too young at that time.'

There were few such perfect days in early autumn. The village was looking its best, the church, so typically English, nestling among trees all changing colour, blazing gold and rust in the warm sunshine. The light had even penetrated the interior of the church, gleaming gently through the stained glass, casting a mellow glow on the packed congregation.

In the porch the three bridesmaids were waiting; the adult was Patrick's sister, Grainne, and the other two were the eight-year-old twin daughters of Leigh's cousin. All were excited and pretty in dresses of cream silk patterned all over with tiny sprigs of flowers.

'Now.' Mrs Gray, churchwarden and general organiser of village affairs, gave a signal. 'She's ready for you now. Off you go and good luck.' Which was what she had been saying to brides for the past twenty years. The music of Wagner's 'Bridal March' began rather wheezily on the organ and Leigh Gregory started at last on the short journey which would transform her into Leigh Cavour.

There he was, at the far end in front of the altar, waiting for her. She could see the back of his head, hair immaculately cut, and beside him, not quite so tall but almost as handsome, his brother Fergal. Both were incredibly distinguished in morning dress.

The front pews were packed—on the one side with Cavours, Gregorys on the other. It was impossible to miss her mother's hat, that enormous affair in dusky pink, abundantly swathed with veiling. How she had enjoyed choosing it.

That had been something of a surprise, discovering how her mother had thrown herself into the rushed preparations with a zest which had been sorely lacking in past years. It was as if she had taken on an entirely fresh lease of life and was relishing the challenge. For example, the day they had spent hunting for the dress, she had refused to allow Leigh to settle for something entirely adequate in the first shop, had selected from a whole row the one she imagined would be perfect for her daughter.

And she had been right. Leigh knew she was wearing the perfect dress... There was no need for the muffled gasps of pleasure to reassure her that it suited her; the mirror back in her bedroom at the vicarage had done just that. She knew she was looking her absolute best, with a faintly dreamy quality which she found fascinating. So much was due to the heavy cream silk, quite gorgeous on its own, but when you added the close-fitting bodice, the scooped neckline and short puffed sleeves, both decorated with seed-pearls, and the skirt, straight and elegant in front, flowing at the back into a short train, it was...well, stunning was not too extravagant a description in this case.

Her first instinct had been against a veil—after all, they'd been aiming for a very simple country wedding—but they had come up against a very slick saleswoman who had urged her to 'try it just for the effect' and then, of course, she had been lost. Yards of sheer silk tulle, falling just as far as the elbows, were gathered into a little bandeau, perfect for the swept-back hairstyle she had had in mind, and now, as she walked slowly through the church, the sun seemed to catch in the cobwebby folds, the shimmering nimbus gathered about her adding to that dreamy air. And in her hand she held the bouquet which Patrick had had delivered that morning—roses, merging through cream and all shades of gold, backed by trails of wispy fern.

Now she was almost there. Her father was preparing to relinquish his place by her side and the elusive scent of Patrick's cologne was all about her as he turned. His eyes were on hers and her heart was behaving in its usual irrational way, was swelling with such joy that for a moment her vision blurred.

But then it cleared; their eyes met and his were tender, hers soft with the perfection of the moment. Her lips parted in what wasn't quite a smile. In his buttonhole was a rose, matching those in her bouquet, in the deepest shade of gold. He just looked, eyes searching her face, lingering for a mischievous moment on her parted lips, then his attention was caught by a glint, moved lower, and there, nestling against her creamy skin, was the beautiful silver chain given nearly six years before, and it was supporting the teardrop crystal.

His eyes were back on her face, were gleaming with that faint secret smile; his hand was reaching out for hers. Fingers linked, together they turned to face the archdeacon.

The meal was over, the speeches—with some witticisms which had made the bride blush and lower her head—made, listened to and applauded with all the uninhibited pleasure that the happy guests could achieve. While a small army of women cleared away the main tables, the cake was cut, further toasts were drunk, and meantime a trio of musicians gathered at the far end of the marquee beside the small dance-floor.

The guests, tongues loosened, formalities dispensed with, began to circulate, apparently by osmosis drifting towards the dance area where tuning up had begun.

'I think they're waiting for us.' Patrick touched his wife's elbow, relieved her of her empty champagne glass. Unseen fingers trailed down the bare skin of her inner arm while she...she had to work hard to disguise the shudder that his touch evoked.

'Darling?' She looked at him questioningly, trying to remember what she and Holly had been discussing.

'I'm sure Holly will excuse us.' And what woman could be impervious to that raised eyebrow, the look which hinted at intimacy? 'Especially when she knows that in a few weeks we'll be neighbours.'

'Yes, get on with you—your guests are waiting. Not that I excuse you for keeping me in the dark for so long, especially when I saw myself in the role of matchmaker. I shall want to know all about it when I see you in Paris.' She looked round as Paul came up, slipped her hand through his arm and sighed happily as they watched the bride and bridegroom thread their way through the crowd and on to the dance-floor.

There, for just a few moments, Patrick and Leigh stood looking at each other, the world forgotten, he with his hands on her waist, hers on his shoulders. In the background the music began softly, softly, an elusive tune, which as it strengthened made them sway together till Patrick took one of her hands in his.

'Remember me?' His mouth curved upwards at the corners. 'Remember me, the guy who waited nearly six long years...?'

'I remember.' Her tone was drowsy. 'Don't forget I'm the girl who waited five years, eight months and six days, but——' she smiled as his arm tightened menacingly '—it seemed every minute of six years.'

And, still gazing intently at each her, Patrick swept her along to the lilting, seductive sound of a Strauss waltz. One or two guests drew closer, and began to clap in time to the music. Others at once took it up, till the pair on the floor were surrounded by a host of well-wishers, but they were so absorbed in each other, they barely noticed.

'How on earth...?' Later that evening they were dancing again, but the venue had changed. Now they were in that country hotel near Oxford which Leigh remembered so well, the sight of which had made her catch her breath as he'd driven in through the gates. 'How on earth did you think of it, Patrick?' she asked him now. 'It's still the same.' She smiled innocently, dazzling the man who was strumming on the double-bass. 'Even the same trio, I swear.'

'You made him miss a note—did you hear? You ought not to smile at men like that.'

'When you stepped on my toe, do you mean?'

She gasped as his arm pulled her even closer, then he whirled her through the door and out into the hall. 'No, that's not what I meant. I'm going to take you away from all this.' Hand in hand, they ran across the hallway, began to climb the curving staircase. 'In our room I've arranged for a bottle of iced champagne, a light supper, and then...'

'And then?' With the door closed behind them she leaned back, linking her hands about his neck. 'And then?' Her lips brushed against his.

'And then I'm going to ask if you're hungry.'

She shook her head. 'Not for food.'

'Or thirsty?' He grinned, as if anticipating her answer.

'Not for wine.'

'But you are...particularly shameless. Confess it.' Which she did, quite willingly.

But later, sitting up in bed, she found that she was both hungry and thirsty, and reached for one of the bite-size sandwiches filled with smoked salmon, sipped at the icy wine. 'Mmm.' She burrowed a little deeper into the pillows. 'I could so easily become used to this.'

'Don't,' he warned, leaning forward to drop a swift kiss on her mouth. 'Don't get too used to it, will you?'

'Oh?' Her heart was hammering again, that wild tattoo which indicated only one thing, and who could be surprised, with that powerful body dressed in nothing but a brief fluffy towel leaning so close to her? Reaching out, she touched his silky skin. 'What do you mean?'

'I mean that——' he caught at her hand, dropped a kiss into the palm '——besides bringing you back here to where it all began, I have other plans which won't provide the same standards of luxury.'

'Oh.' Now there was a faint frown as she tried to follow. 'But I thought it was New York, then Vermont.'

'It is. And I promise it's going to be luxury all the way to Vermont, but after that...'

'Patrick.' Sensing some drama, she put down her glass, and without thinking knelt in the tumbled bed, took his hand and held it against her. 'Please, tell me what you mean.'

'You realise——' he moved his hand a little '—if this continues I shan't be able to tell you anything much.' He grinned. 'I shall be forced to take action.'

'Oh.' She reached for the wisp of lace masquerading as a nightdress. 'Is that better?'

'Much,' he said sardonically, then recognised signs of impatience. 'You know I've always regretted that we didn't spend those years in Ashala together.' Taking her almost imperceptible nod for agreement, he went on. 'What would you say if I told you we were going back there?'

'Patrick?' Idly she reached for the narrow strap which had slipped down her shoulder. 'Ashala?'

'Mmm.' How closely he was watching her. 'What would you say?'

'I'd say... how wonderful. I want to see the sun setting on the Ganges, bathing it in a golden haze.' She was gently mocking. 'So long as I see it with you.'

'Impudence.' He grinned. 'But I don't think I said the Ganges, just one of the tributaries, and I promise I'll be there with you. And it's just for a few days. When I left they made me promise I would take my wife there one day. And, since I didn't imagine I would ever marry, it was easy enough to make that promise. But... you're sure you don't mind?'

'I'm quite sure. Rather the reverse, in fact.'

'Good. You see, I still haven't quite recovered from the shock of your refusal first time round. You've no idea what it did to my ego.'

'Mmm, strange—I've never noticed the least thing lacking in your ego.' She giggled when he made a threatening move, uncurled herself from the bed and strolled across the expanse of pale carpet to study her reflection, blushing at the skimpiness of the garment she was wearing. 'What——' her face was burning '—do you think of this...? Do you prefer it to the wedding-dress?' Their eyes met in the mirror as he came to stand behind her; he was smiling and it was hard not to respond.

'Well.' His fingers touched the narrow strap, skimmed over the lacy top. 'I suppose each has its place.' He appeared to consider. 'Put it this way; if you had come up the aisle dressed as you are right now, I should have been surprised, maybe even a little bit...embarrassed.'

'Would you, now?' She turned and was immediately imprisoned. 'And if I had found *you* waiting for me dressed like *that*, do you know what I would have done?' All at once her control lapsed; she was smiling, then they were both laughing and he was carrying her back to the bed.

'Go on,' he challenged, his mouth very close to hers. 'Tell me what you would have done. Surprise me.'

'I think...' She raked her fingers through his hair. 'I think I might have done something very much like...this.' Her lips parted, her breath mingling with his.

'Right there?' It was a moment later, and he sounded as if he had been running. 'In front of the congregation?'

'No.' She shook her head and the dark, silky mass of hair spread out over the pillow. 'No, I should have asked the archdeacon if he would excuse us for just a few moments.'

'Not enough.' He slipped one arm beneath her, raising her body towards his. 'Not nearly enough. You see . . . it's going to take the rest of our lives.'

Harlequin Romance ®

New from Harlequin Romance
a very special six-book series by

MIDNIGHT SONS

DEBBIE MACOMBER

The town of Hard Luck, Alaska, needs women!

The O'Halloran brothers, who run a bush-plane service called Midnight Sons, are heading a campaign to attract women to Hard Luck. *(Location: north of the Arctic Circle. Population: 150—mostly men!)*

"Debbie Macomber's *Midnight Sons* series is a delightful romantic saga. And each book is a powerful, engaging story in its own right. Unforgettable!"
—Linda Lael Miller

TITLE IN THE MIDNIGHT SONS SERIES:

Harlequin Romance ®

brings you
a special Valentine's treat!

How the West was wooed!

Let Harlequin Romance take you back to the ranch
with Hitched! our all new rodeo of romance, featuring
rugged, handsome, one hundred percent cowboy
heroes who are about to discover just how the West
was wooed!

February brings TO LASSO A LADY (#3397)
by Renee Roszel, featuring a special Valentine roundup
straight from the heart of Wyoming. Amy Vale was
determined to be the best rancher's wife ever! She'd
found someone nice to spend her life with; someone
honest who could make her smile. Passion, as far as
Amy was concerned, was overrated.

Beau Diablo, Amy's future stepson, certainly lived up to
his name. He was one sexy cowboy. Beau was not going
to let his father make a fool of himself over some blonde
bimbo from the big city. He was going to put a stop to
this marriage. And he knew just how to do it!

Beau's sizzling kisses were hot enough to melt all the
snow in the state. He knew just how to steal a woman's
heart—and Valentine's Day seemed the right time to
do it!

"A sassy, fun read!"
Curtiss Ann Matlock

UNLOCK THE DOOR TO GREAT ROMANCE AT BRIDE'S BAY RESORT

Join Harlequin's new across-the-lines series, set in an exclusive hotel on an island off the coast of South Carolina.

Seven of your favorite authors will bring you exciting stories about fascinating heroes and heroines discovering love at Bride's Bay Resort.

Look for these fabulous stories coming to a store near you beginning in January 1996.

Harlequin American Romance #613 in January
Matchmaking Baby by Cathy Gillen Thacker

Harlequin Presents #1794 in February
Indiscretions by Robyn Donald

Harlequin Intrigue #362 in March
Love and Lies by Dawn Stewardson

Harlequin Romance #3404 in April
Make Believe Engagement by Day Leclaire

Harlequin Temptation #588 in May
Stranger in the Night by Roseanne Williams

Harlequin Superromance #695 in June
Married to a Stranger by Connie Bennett

Harlequin Historicals #324 in July
Dulcie's Gift by Ruth Langan

Visit Bride's Bay Resort each month wherever Harlequin books are sold.

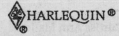

HARLEQUIN®

BBAYG

HARLEQUIN PRESENTS®

Harlequin brings you the best books, by the best authors!

MIRANDA LEE

"...another scandalously sensual winner"
—*Romantic Times*

&

LYNNE GRAHAM

"(Her) strong-willed, hard-loving characters are the sensual stuff dreams are made of"—*Romantic Times*

Look out next month for:

MISTRESS OF DECEPTION by Miranda Lee
Harlequin Presents #1791

CRIME OF PASSION by Lynne Graham
Harlequin Presents #1792

Harlequin Presents—the best has just gotten better!
Available in February wherever Harlequin books are sold.

TAUTH-5